A Different Continuum

Early Tales of Imagination

by Gary Gentile

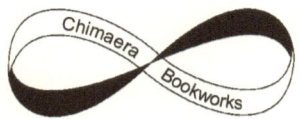

Chimaera Bookworks
P.O. Box 57137
Philadelphia, PA 19111

Additional copies of this book may be purchased from the same address by sending a check or money order in the amount of $15 U.S. for each copy (plus $4 postage per order, not per book, in the U.S. Inquire for shipping cost to foreign countries). Alternatively, copies may be purchased from the author's website, and paid by credit card:

http://www.ggentile.com

Cover art by Wolf Simone

International Standard Book Numbers (ISBN)
1-883056-32-2
978-1-883056-32-2

First Edition

Printed in the U.S.A.

CONTENTS

PREFACE

In the Preface to my first short story collection, *A Different Universe,* I described the circumstances that initiated my life-long interest in writing. I must repeat some of that background information, and expand it in order to introduce the stories that are contained in the present collection.

When I was sixteen years old, my eleventh-grade English teacher (whose name I have long-since forgotten) offered to raise each student's grade by one letter if he or she wrote an essay, short story, or poem.

By that time in my life, I had been reading science fiction books for a couple of years, as recreation. I was excited by the action, adventure, and imaginative scope that were science fiction's hallmarks.

I studied hard to improve my grades. My teacher's proposal presented the perfect opportunity, not only to get a better report card, but to test my creative skills. I was inspired to write a science fiction story that was based upon my own original concept.

The result was "The Nothing." I wrote the story in long hand. My mother, who worked in a bank as a private secretary, typed it for me. The typewritten manuscript ran to 47 pages. The teacher probably would have raised my grade from a B to an A only for the amount of effort that I put into the project. He told me that never in his experience had a student written anything as long.

In front of the class, he announced that he was amazed not only by the elegance of my expression, but by the originality of my ideas and the associated plot device (or words to that effect). I was thrilled by his commendation. In addition, he told me that over summer vacation, he was going to show my story to a friend who was a professional science fiction writer. The author's name was Lester Del Ray.

I had read some of Del Ray's science fiction, so I was aware of how well he was respected in the field. I was excited by the prospect of having my work seen and critiqued by a professional in the business. I entertained thoughts of becoming a fulltime science fiction author after completing my education. This inspired me to write other stories – not for school credit, but just for my own edification, so I could work my craft, and perhaps to have some other stories to show to Del Ray.

In those days, each grade consisted of two semesters: A and B. One semester ran from the beginning of September to the third week in January; the other semester ran from the end of January to the third week of June. Also in those days, one could start school in January instead of in September. Because I started first grade in January (at the age of five and a half, I graduated from 11A when summer vacation began.

I eagerly anticipated meeting my English teacher again when I entered 11B that autumn. I was deflated to learn, however, that he had never contacted Del Ray that summer. A great opportunity for early recognition was lost to me. This put a decided damper on my enthusiasm, but nonetheless I kept creating and developing ideas, and occasionally putting them down on paper.

Fifteen years after graduating from high school – and after a convoluted path through college, the Army, service in Vietnam, and an occupation in construction, I retired from the electrical union to become a fulltime author. Writing has been my passion ever since. By now I have written fifty-one books and numerous short stories and articles.

Saver that I am, I kept my pre-professional works in a folder throughout the years. The present book collects these teenage stories, which are arranged in chronological sequence. I have reread these stories now for the first time since I wrote them. Although they do not possess the sophistication of my later professional works, they have a verve and freshness about them that forecasts the author that I was eventually to become.

True science fiction differs from other forms of literature by being imaginative and thought-provoking. It may contain social commentary. My early stories possess these qualities as much as my professionally written stories of a couple of decades later.

If I were to assign a title to "Destruction" today, I would call it "Perspective." I have placed that title in parentheses, in order to differentiate it from the original title that I gave it as a teenager.

All too often, an author's early works are not collected or published until after his demise. I have decided not to wait that long before making my early stories available to my readers.

In separate volumes, I am also making available my two early novels: *A Journey to the Center of the Earth*, and *The Mold*. I wrote the former during summer vacation between 12A and 12B. I wrote the latter after graduating high school in January 1964, and before entering college the following September. (Temple University did not have split semesters.)

After graduation from high school, I took a two-week typing course at a local business school, in anticipation of needing to type reports and papers in college.

After getting drafted between semesters, I did not write or type again until 1976, when I started my plan to retire from the construction field, in order to commence my new career as an author. This transition lasted for three years, during which time I was unemployed for months at a time. In order to prepare for my new career, I bought an electric typewriter and a typing instruction manual, and taught myself how to type again. At night, after work, I plunked away at the keyboard until I achieved some sense of proficiency in touch-typing. In 1979, I officially retired permanently from the union.

When I examined my old files in order to prepare the present collection, I found a term paper that I wrote for my college English class. I know that my teacher's name was Mr. Goldberg because his name was typed on the cover page. He gave his students an assignment to write a term paper on any subject that appealed to them. Because I was a science major, and had a long and abiding interest in all scientific pursuits, I chose astronomy as my topic. The purpose of the paper was not so much to prove a point as to teach us how to conduct research by using library services. I learned this lesson extremely well, for in addition to my career in science fiction, I became an historian and the author of more than thirty history books (so far).

I received an A- for the paper. Goldberg graded it minus not because I did not do adequate research and reach a valid scientific conclusion, but because of the length of the paper: it was too long. He wanted an eight-page paper. The only way that I could squeeze all my research into ten pages was by having no margins on the top, bottom, and right sides of the pages, and by typing in elite font (which has twelve characters per linear inch instead of ten characters per inch, as in pica, which was the standard font). I was trying to trick Goldberg into not noticing that the paper was much longer than it was supposed to be.

My bibliography and list of sources were also more extensive than he wanted. However, I found it impossible to edit the paper to a shorter length because all my research materials were necessary in order to establish the validity of my conclusions.

In discussing the paper, he mentioned its length as exceeding his parameters, but in such a way that I had the impression that he secretly admired the depth of my research.

Because I had space available between these covers, I have included "The Possibilities of Life on Venus" as an example of my early nonfiction writing.

Also in my old files, I found two short stories that I never completed. That is, I wrote a complete rough draft of each one, then wrote a second draft, and made notations for the third and final draft, which I never got around to writing (until now).

I did not apply a title to the first of these stories. It appears here as "Untitled." In parentheses, I have offered a title which, in retrospect, I think is fitting: "The Other World."

Neither story was dated. I usually did not put a date on the folder until after completion. Although I was writing professionally fulltime when I commenced these stories, I did not apply the final polish and type them on unmarked paper. I put them aside and went on to other projects, after which these stories lay fallow.

Because "Untitled" was typed on the same kind of paper on which I typed other contemporaneous stories, I inferred that I wrote the first two drafts around 1980.

The other short story was entitled "The Eyes of the Beholder." Although there was no date associated with this story, I typed it on the back of a rough draft of *Return to Mars*. Because I completed that novel in 1982, I inferred that I wrote the first and second drafts of this short story at about the same time, after I no longer needed the rough draft of the novel. I was broke in those days, so I utilized every resource at my disposal to continue my writing career, instead of returning to electrical work. I saved every sheet of paper that had a blank side, including circulars and advertising papers that I received in the mail.

While neither "The Other World" nor "The Eyes of the Beholder" are early works, I have included them in the present collection – not just because there is space for them, but so they will not become lost forever, or end up being stored in some musty library that inherits my manuscripts, in which case they might never be read or made available to the public.

THE NOTHING

The laboratory was big. It covered an area equal to a square city block. It was situated on the mesa of a steep hill, which was so common in Texas. The two smaller buildings to the north were also part of the massive laboratory, but their function was wholly different. One was a large motel which housed many of the scientists who did not have private homes. The other was a warehouse.

It was the only scientific laboratory in the world that was completely devoted to the study of cosmic radiation. Its millionaire owner, 55-year-old Tom Parley was alone in the awesome place that night. He was hunched over some illegible notes which were scattered over the table before him.

Sleepily he rubbed his eyes. He rose from his chair and cast a surreptitious glance at the semi-global superimposed cosmic radiation recorder. The great continent of North America was outlined under the plastic screen. It covered the total expanse from the northern islands of Canada to part of Venezuela and Columbia in South America, stretching laterally as far as 55° longitude in the North Atlantic and 140° longitude in the North Pacific. Over this circular, four-foot-diameter map lay the detective apparatus for the super-abundance of cosmic radiation bombardment, turned to the same scale as the map. Thus, when an unusual amount of cosmic radiation occurred, the viewer could see exactly where. A series of small bulbs underlined the map so that they lit up the area of acute crop-ups; a buzzer was also attached to the equipment.

Parley ambled to a processing data machine and yanked out some ten feet of recording tape. Jagged lines jumped high to show him when and where cosmic radiation bombardment was at a maximum. He and his competent staff were trying to correlate large amounts of cosmic phenomena with sun spot maxima, novae, supernovae, and so on. But as yet there were no correlations even in the most fantastic way.

As he concentrated on the tape, he meandered to the large picture window. Through it, several miles distant, the lights of Dallas shone brightly. He checked his gaze and peered up at the black, nighttime void. Because of heat inversions the sky seemed to waver in soft, oscillating motions and the stars flickered relentlessly.

Suddenly a buzzer sounded loudly. He dropped the tape and ran to the machine. Parley thumbed the button that would turn off the buzzer while he scanned the screen. His attention was immediately grasped by the glow of the bulb under the screen. Even as he looked, that bulb went off and another came on as the position of bombardment advanced.

But what he saw, what the machine detected, was an impossibility. Normally there was radiation everywhere, at every time, despite Terran or stellar conditions. However, he saw something that made him look twice - three times. For the scanner had picked up a pocket of nothing. An absolutely empty space moved over the screen across Venezuela. The reason the buzzer had sounded was that as the great pocket moved it pushed waves of radiation out of its way, causing intense radiation to gather behind and on both sides of it.

Parley could do nothing but watch. The machine recorded the exact time (sidereal and local), pinpointed the exact location, and plotted the apparent path. He glowered at the cosmic prodigy, his heart pounding furiously at the excitement. He was watching an extraordinary event in the history of scientific knowledge. Perhaps there was a means by which he might learn the reason for the anti-radiation shield and perfect one for use on spaceships. The possibilities were infinite, but so were the probabilities.

He gripped the sides of the table. The one defect in the machine was that it was merely two dimensional, and the height was not shown. The pocket was definitely in the atmosphere, of that he could be sure, but he could only conjecture as to its altitude.

Parley mostly wanted to know how the thing was going to end, since he had never seen anything like it before. It was dangerously close to the edge of the screen, and with each flick of the bulb, its proximity increased. He became impatient for the end. The whole experience had only lasted for fifteen seconds so far, but to him it seemed like an incredibly long time.

The pocket flitted slowly over Venezuela, but in reality it must have been moving at hundreds of miles an hour over the dense South American jungle. Hopefully he watched and waited. It was just at the limit of his cosmic radiation detector when the last bulb flickered out and the screen went dead.

*   *   *   *   *

It had been an ordinary, hot, blistering, summer day in San Vilaga, Venezuela. The sun had been bright and fiery, the atmosphere arid and sticky, the people warm and lethargic. But still they continued their work meticulously, seeking out the coolest spots of sympathetic shade. The little village was less than five hundred miles from the equator.

The total population of the village (more properly, family, since every one of its clansmen were somehow interrelated) was less then two hundred, a number to which one had recently been added. Fredona and his handsome wife, Lorba, had already conceived two sons; Pedro was eleven and Chico was five. Both boys were very exuberant about having a little sister.

The day was also festive in their household because they were preparing for the party that night, celebrating the latest addition. There was not really too much preparing, since everyone brought food and distributed it evenly, but meager decorations were set up and tables and chairs borrowed.

Night came, and the fun had just begun. Lorba had to tend the baby, but found plenty of help. She had promised her two boys that they would be allowed to stay up for the occasion, but Chico had graciously crawled into his crib, of which he was soon to be relieved, and Pedro lingered on hopefully, just to be around.

People milled around the several fires, and chattered against the background of assorted nighttime sounds from the nearby jungle. The fortunate pair accepted many overt congratulations from the relatives and several friends from the nearby villages.

Abruptly the nighttime sky was brought into full, almost daylike illumination by a descending, glowing orb. It mounted the sky like a beacon as it labored through the thick stratosphere. The simple people recognized it as a shooting star: an extraordinarily huge meteor which, by friction of the molecules comprising the air, burnt brilliantly in its path toward the ground.

Every eye was watching the display, but few looked directly at it, for it was so exhaustingly bright that they had to shield their eyes from it protectively with their hands.

Pedro was now wide awake, brought to arousal first by the sparkling ball of luminance and then by the screams and utterances. It persisted for perhaps fifteen full seconds before it was blocked out by the trees of the jungle. Then, at least twenty seconds later a resounding crash was heard from away off in the distance.

Instantly there was darkness, and for a short while, the visual purple having been completely bleached, the people were blinded by the absolute obfuscation.

*   *   *   *   *

The morning after the party, Pedro got up early. He had decided to go fishing today. He knew of a special spot which his father had used when he was a boy. The fish always bit exceedingly well in the shaded oasis.

He walked around the house on tiptoe so as not to wake his parents. After eating a hasty breakfast he prepared a large lunch, collected his fishing accessories (a bamboo pole, adorned with store-bought string and hooks) and dug up some worms and beetles from under a rotting log. Within twenty minutes he was skipping merrily along a clear jungle path. When his mother saw that his bamboo pole was not it its proper place, she would take it as a signal that he would not be home until shortly after lunchtime, as Pedro usually ate his lunch early and came home starving.

It was at least two miles distant to his fishing spot, but he loved the jungle so that he did not mind walking - or running, as was the case most of the time. The early morning was cool, but by running feverishly his body circulated just enough blood to compensate for it comfortably. As it happened, Pedro arrived at his destination in just under a half hour.

He hung his lunch on a branch from a greased string, so as to discourage ravenous pismires from eating it. Pedro hardly noticed the absence of life in the jungle, for he took it as a matter of course. He did not notice that no animals ran from his onslaught. He did not notice that no pesky insects swarmed above and about his face. But after fishing for a half hour he did notice there were no fish nibbling at his hook. Then he took notice of the morbid serenity of his surroundings.

Vividly he remembered the beautiful spectacle of the previous night. The giant fireball had come, spitting and sputtering, almost overhead. He wondered if, for some reason, that was the cause of the queerness (that was the only word that would describe it) of the jungle today. What possible bearing it might have had eluded him, but he made up his mind to explore the jungle deeper, and to hunt for it.

Determinedly he set off through the jungle, leaving his fishing equipment stacked under his lunch. He walked on, the soundlessness ringing in his ears from psychological tympanic vibration, the only noise being that of the snapping vegetation under his sandals and the whispering of a slight breeze through the treetops.

Pedro made very little progress, for often he found himself walking very slowly and glancing around over his shoulder. He could not bring himself to speed up, for the whole jungle seemed ominous. Its lifelessness was astounding, and several times he jumped up at the slight sound of the cracking of a twig underfoot.

He grew very tired from his crouched stance; his shoulders ached incessantly. But soon he knew that he was near the resting place of the meteorite. The tops of the tallest trees had-been sheered off and the stubs burnt. Since the path of the meteor had been oblique it was not long before he had come considerably close. There was a raised hill, and the trees had been sheered off almost to the ground at the apex. The meteorite, then, lay just over the crest.

He broke into a stumbled run and climbed the hill. He got to the top and stood to his full height. The sight that greeted him was not anything like he had expected. He thought that he would find a large, burnt stone lying in the jungle; but *this*, this was totally unreal.

An area about two thousand feet across had been completely flattened. Most of it consisted of fallen trees and brush which seemed to be wrinkled and had an unnatural shade of brown. At the very center of this devastation was a small patch of charred vegetation approximately two hundred feet in diameter. And in the middle of *that* there lay a pockmarked rock as big as a house, of which only half was above ground. To Pedro this was fantastically big. But he did not realize that a meteorite of that size should have created a blast area a hundred, a thousand times larger. Whether his thoughts were anywhere between fright and abject horror, or from thoughtfulness to astonishment, it did not show itself in his featureless, blank face.

And worst of all, there was no movement.

Just a thick cloud of wonder pervaded his simple mind. He had never known of such things as this, had never had a chance to. So he stood there with a drooping lower jaw, feeling, sensing the shroud of evil that blanketed the space.

There came a sudden crashing sound, and Pedro choked on a gasp lodged in his throat. He saw a tall tree wither, turn brown, and topple over, taking a second in it flight. It took several other resounding crashes before he took account of what was happening. He did not look at any one place in particular, but just stared off wildly at the clearing. Because of this he gained an overall perspective and saw that the outer periphery of the circle of death was moving outward in all directions, in three hundred sixty degrees.

With this insight he turned and ran in stark fear. He weaved his way around large holes, but became reckless of the tangling underbrush. All he could think of was that death was after him. Because of his care-lessness he soon tripped over a stray log and tumbled over; pain reached up and down his leg. He disregard-ed it and tried to get up, but he had lost all power of mobility in that leg. So he crawled.

He whipped his head around and saw the entire jungle collapsing around him. It came straight for him, and he was helpless. Large trees toppled everywhere, one just narrowly missing-him. The vines, grass, and small bushes suffered the same fate of withering, browning, and dying. In desperation he grabbed the ground and pulled himself forward. But he was too late. The advancing circle of death caught up with him. Sud-denly his muscles felt drained of their strength, and he could no longer think. His life forces were being tapped, drawn right out of him.

He collapsed.

He would never rise again.

*   *   *   *   *

Back at home Lorba was getting worried. It would be dark in another hour. Pedro had never stayed out this late before, since he usually did what his stomach directed. Lorba put down her daughter and leaned out the door. "Where is that son of ours? It is late and he is not back yet." she called out to Fredona, who was chop-ping wood near the edge of the jungle.

"Do not worry," he assured her. "Perhaps the fish-ing was very good and he lost track of time. Soon he will come home with a full string of fish for tomorrow's dinner."

"And if he does, who will clean them?" she retorted, then stalked back into the house to the waiting baby.

Fredona took only half a dozen strong strokes when Francisco marched dejectedly out of the jungle, his rifle loose in his grasp. He shouted, "Hail Francisco! How was hunting?"

"I've never seen such a day as this," muttered Francisco, who was obviously tired from a long day's walk. "Not one sign of wildlife have I seen today. After a long day's hunting I have come home empty handed. Never before has this happened."

"What is the world coming to?" sighed Fredona.

Francisco ignored him and went on. "There is something wrong in the jungle today. I did not even have occasion to fire my gun. See, I still have my first bullet in the chamber. Even the insects have disappeared." ("True," inserted Fredona.) "And the silence is unbearable" ("Indeed, an omen," said Fredona.) "And there are no fish in the water - "

"What?" yelled Fredona.

"Oh, to be sure, there are many in the water, but they are all belly up."

Lorba stepped outside again. "Hail, Francisco. Have you seen my boy today?"

But Fredona did not give him time to answer. Instead, he said, "Francisco, will you come with me to look for my son?" He explained the situation, then: "Now, with your bad news I can only fear the worst."

"Surely, but it will be dark soon."

"I will get some torches." He disappeared into the house and was out almost immediately. "I will hurry back, Lorba."

"Be careful," she called, but they were already in the jungle, hurrying down the path.

They went in silence, not caring to make a noise in the dead jungle. Even through the small remnant of instinct left in them, it was very apparent that all was not well. Not even a breeze blew. The two men arrived at the fishing hole in double time, and, after seeing

Pedro's lunch still there in its entirety, they continued on, picking up the trail which the small boy had not tried to conceal.

After they saw that the trail followed a perfectly straight line, they hardly bothered to pick up every clue; they just checked every few minutes. Fredona whispered something to the effect of, "The boy should never have come this far alone."

They followed the trail for many minutes, finally finding the blazed path in the treetops by the last glimmering rays of the sun. Fredona lit the two torches and gave one to Francisco. Immediately following they saw the circle of death ahead, much larger than it had been this morning. Slowly but deliberately they mounted a fallen tree trunk and inspected the area from the slight vantage point. Never had they seen such a disturbing sight as this.

It was so dark that the meteorite was not visible, but Francisco had foresight: "Could the falling star have done this and perhaps be the cause of all our trouble? We know not what terrific forces it contained."

Fredona kneeled and held his torch low. "I have seen dead rabbits before, but none like this." He was surveying an abandoned litter of newly born rabbits. He shuddered at the sight of the four little hares, frozen into weird positions by their last death throes. They did not have a putrid odor, but the appearance was horrible, enhanced by the withered and shriveled look. They certainly looked dead, but it was not a natural state of death. The whole thing was unexplainable.

Falteringly Fredona took a step forward; then another; and another.

"Pedro is in here. I know it." What is the sixth sense that tells people things that they have no reason to believe? Whatever it was, it was at work here.

Francisco, terrified beyond belief, wanted to leave. But he could not quit on his friend. So he too continued the search. As encouragement he said aloud, "But surely the small boy would be more frightened than we. He would not stay here." He felt no shame or effeminacy in admitting to his fear.

"My son is in here," shouted the enraged father.

"Please," pleaded Francisco. "Let us go." He was thinking more of his own safety than he was of the boy.

"I must find him."

"But it is dark. You can not . . . " His voice flowed into a gasp as Fredona stopped and glared at an indistinct shape lying supine on the ground.

Suddenly Fredona was back in his senses. He fell to his knees and whispered, "Pedro." No answer. "Pedro." He shook his shoulder. Pedro lay on his stomach so that Fredona could not see him well. Fredona grabbed the boy's shoulder and quickly rolled him over.

Such a horrible sight was never to be seen. Pedro's face was contorted in fear; even that was visible through the loose folds of skin which hung on tenaciously to a dead skull. The eyes were sunk deep into the sockets, no longer supported by the full mass of the brain. The nose was a flap of skin that fell to one side.

Francisco screamed, retreated a few steps, and crashed into a failed tree. Fredona simply hung his head low and cried; nor was he ashamed. Finally he got enough nerve to lift the body and stand. It was horrible to the touch. So repulsive was it, in fact, that Fredona hardly wanted to admit that it was indeed his son. Francisco came back and picked up the dropped torches. After touching them to some surrounding vines, he saw that the dead vegetation did not burn. This was another oddity to add up and account for.

Walking like a zombie, Fredona tramped through the forest, carrying his encumbrance in his folded arms. Without saying a word or uttering a sound, he walked the many miles home without changing his position. Determination was set in his muscles.

They arrived at the village and Lorba, alerted of their coming by the two burning torches, ran out of the house hopefully. But when she saw Pedro in his father's arms and his lachrymose expression, she screamed and clung to Fredona, definitely afraid of the body.

Francisco was left outside alone, to do the explaining. Many people gathered around and stabbed at him with questions, but for a long time he could say nothing.

*   *   *   *   *

Rick Hunter drove into the hamlet the next day. He expected to be flooded with requests for his wares. He drove an old World War Two, United States Army surplus truck; he had had it for several years. When he had gotten into the lucrative business of selling much-wanted merchandise to the remote villages in Venezuela, he had expected to start a business consisting of many trucks. But things had not worked out the way he planned. Sure, he had a sizable bank account, but not enough to sustain another truck. He had wanted to get out of the business for several months but he knew nothing else. So he was stuck.

Hunter became very worried when he drove down the main street (a wide dirt path lined by huts on both sides) and saw the emptiness of everything. He chugged along to the emporium and parked, but no happy faces rushed up to greet him; no crowds pushed, and pulled to see the new things that he had brought for trade. He just sat in his truck wondering. A passing thought flitted through his mind: a job like this is more philanthropic than lucrative.

On a sudden idea he gunned the motor and took off down the street. He was out of the town in about ten seconds, but he headed down a narrow jungle path, barely large enough for the truck. Soon the path led to a small llano which the villagers used as a cemetery. The entire village seemed to be congregated at the far end of the clearing. Hunter reasoned that it must be a funeral.

He drove across the gleaming grass and braked his truck to a halt about fifty feet from the farthest extent of the crowd. Several people glanced up at his imposing figure (he stood six feet two inches in height), but mostly they whispered among each other and looked forlorn and shook their heads, saying words like, "It is a shame," or something similar.

Hunter pushed his way through the crowd, exchanging greetings. Finally he saw a great multitude listening to one speaker. The people huddled around so close that Hunter could hardly hear, but he managed to pick up some words - words enough to get the general idea of the situation. He was amazed. He had only gotten dribs and drabs, but it was enough to whet his curiosity.

Just then a small procession marched down the path. Four men bore a hastily made casket, followed by the bereaved family and some of the closest relatives. They lined up in front of the grave, every head down. The spectators lowered their heads in reverence while they went through the ritual of liturgy over the casket. As the casket was being lowered, a rumbling seemed to come from deep within the jungle. Many heads broke from reverence and stared off into the trees.

At first the people just looked deep into the forest, listening intently.

As the rumbling neared, it had the distinct sound of crashing trees. Off into the hazy distance, Hunter saw a tall tree shudder in the air and then keel over. Seconds later the sound was heard. The air was filled with evaporating dew, and although the immense cloudless sky was beautiful with blue and sunlight, in the distance there was an unmistakable horror.

Someone shouted words into the air and the entire crowd stampeded away from there. The casket was unceremoniously dropped into the hole for which it had been intended and the pallbearers ran. Hunter sensed that something was wrong so he ran to his truck and swerved it around before the mass of people reached him. He did not take off, but rather went slowly so that some of the villagers could climb into the truck. He shouted and waved his hand out the window and motioned some people into the back. When he thought it was about full he pushed the gasoline pedal to the floor and roared away. As he did so he passed several swift runners, one of whom leaped onto the running board and climbed into the cab. When he was in, Hunter blasted out of there and raced through the narrow path. In hardly any time he was racing along the main street of the abandoned village. Then he was out and jogging along a cow path at fifty miles per hour. The trees were so close on both sides that he could reach out and touch them.

Pots and pans and various other utensils crashed around in the back of the truck, giving the passengers a hard time. Many fell out leaving a trail along the road. But he was fleeing for his life; at least he got that impression from the way people were running crazily. He thought of all the poor people left behind to be crushed by the falling trees. But that was the least of it. What could possibly do such a thing? What kind of disease or plague was after them? Rick Hunter then found out that he did not even know why he was running.

Too late he remembered the treacherous curve ahead. The road suddenly veered sharp left and the truck was in danger of turning over. The left side of the truck was fully three feet off the ground. To make matters worse, the front wheel that was still on the ground hit a rock and bounced upward and for a second the entire weight of the truck and passengers rested tenaciously on one wheel. But with all the maneuverability gone from the truck, since he had no steering power, it glanced into a tree. The slight jolt bounced the truck onto all its wheels again and by some odd quirk of fate had faced in the direction of the open road. Hardly knowing what had happened in that instant, Hunter kept the truck going full speed.

After Hunter took the right fork in the road that led to Tarvar village, and then out into semi-civilized country, the road widened somewhat. At least now he was able to put his elbow out of the window and not have it chopped off. Then he noticed that the man in the cab with him was Francisco. Hunter pleaded with him to relate what was wrong, and after much persuading urged him to talk. Whereas Francisco had been jabbering freely before, he was now a scared man in fear of his life. But he finally told everything. Then Rick Hunter was glad that he had left the laniary behind and saved his life along with some of the other frightened people.

He reached Tarvar village in a few minutes. This was a town, larger than San Vilaga, which depended almost solely on fishing. It was the least peopled settlement until Paragua.

Hunter did not exactly know what he was going to do here. He had to warn the people, of that he was sure. But he did not know how. When he arrived and the people (mostly women and children and old men, since the young men were fishing) gathered around, in desperation he got an idea. He pushed Francisco out of the truck, and, after ordering the San Vilaga folk to stay put in the truck, helped him onto the roof. There Francisco related his tale. The effect was terrific. Immediately many people ran into their hovels and began packing some simple belongings. The fishermen were called in and within fifteen minutes the entire village was on the move.

But Rick Hunter did not wait that long. Soon after Francisco had finished his speech, a deluge of monkeys, wild boars, pacas, and other assorted animals trampled through the village. This was a pretty sure sign that the plague was coming rapidly. This was the ultimate climax which really started people running, including Rick Hunter.

He roared out of the village and down the dirt road. He could not dodge all the animals, but he tried to avoid the larger ones. In several minutes he had passed the increasing wave of animals. He pushed his truck to the limit. His purpose was not just to save his own life, but to warn the world of the onslaught. In Paragua he would go to the newspaper office, the editor of which was an old friend, and tell him to send out a general alarm. All this formulated in his mind, but when he came to, "Then what?" he was stuck. Well, he thought, I will just have to wait and see.

About this time in his reasoning he reached the main highway. It was only two lanes wide, but out in the jungle it was called main. From here to Paragua was a hundred miles of smooth riding, and since he was traveling at seventy-five miles per hour, he figured roughly an hour and twenty minutes before he reached his destination.

The next hundred miles passed slowly and uneventfully, except for some cars which he had met, all going in the opposite direction. But Rick Hunter did not give them a second thought. He just drove on. Soon Paragua could be seen in the distance, and before he knew it he was bearing down the city streets. He eased up on the pedal, not so much as to avoid a ticket (law enforcement here was very poor) rather than to avert an accident. Now that he was so close to his destination he could not afford to be killed. It was funny the way he thought of death at that moment. He cared not whether he lived or died, but he must get his urgent message across to the world. He would profit, and not the world, by his death. He forced such morbid thoughts from his mind.

Hunter pulled up in front of the newspaper office. From here one would hardly think that a scant two miles away rose a jungle dense with underbrush. The air-conditioned coolness caught Rick Hunter unawares, but he quickly adjusted. He boarded an elevator and rode to the top floor. Then he marched into the office and said gruffly to the receptionist:

"Tell Tokay that Rick Hunter is here with important news."

She eyed him speculatively, but after a second's hesitation announced that "a rather shabby looking fellow named Hunter" was awaiting audience. It had not occurred to him what a frightful mess he must look like, but at the moment he was not moved by his lack of decor. Some execrable words were shouted over the intercom and with a changed expression the girl said effeminately, "Please go right in, sir." The last word had been tacked on with obvious resentment. But he quickly forgot the impertinent and impetuous secretary and strode into the office.

"You are indeed shabby," said Tokay whimsically.

"I haven't got time for formalities," said Rick. "What I've got to say can't wait for tidiness. The reason I'm here is because you have connections and can get help fast. No, don't interrupt. I just came from the bush country and there is a terrible disaster going on there. There is a plague so large and so communicable that it kills everything it touches. I got out just in time, but I know a couple of hundred villagers who didn't."

"Is it that bad?" asked Tokay

"That bad and worse. You've just got to believe me and get on that phone fast before the plague takes over the . . . " He stopped short. He did not want to let out too much, for if he told the whole absurdity of the thing he would never be believed. He had to let on that it was just a simple, but terrible, plague.

Tokay ignored the dropped sentence and asked, "Do you have any idea of how much damage it has done or how widespread it is?"

"The damage done is indeterminable, and by now it's covered scores of square miles. And it's advancing faster and reaching farther with each minute of delay."

"How do you know this?" Tokay was searching for something that Rick Hunter was not about to divulge.

"I saw it coming," said Hunter too frankly.

"You . . . you saw it coming?" This gave Tokay the opening he wanted.

"No, no, I heard it coming first. I mean, I heard about it. Look, if you don't believe me I've got ten witnesses outside in my truck who can back up my story.

"Oh, that is quite alright."

"Then get on that phone and get help. We haven't got much time." On that he spun on his heel and stalked out of the office. As he passed the secretary she put on a sweet, but false, smile. Rick Hunter slammed the door but did not walk away. He listened through the keyhole.

" . . . Caracas, Emergency Health Department . . . " So he was calling the Capital of Venezuela. The old man had come through.

Rick Hunter quickly made his way outside. He walked around the front of the truck and was about to climb in when he noticed that Francisco was not in the cab. He walked around to the back and peered inside. No one was there. They had deserted him, the poor ignorant fools. But perhaps that was to his advantage. He made up his mind what he was going to do.

First he stopped at the bank and wasted ten minutes closing his account. He stuffed all the cash in his wallet. Then he drove to the warehouse. Mack Handler, the owner, was the man from whom Hunter bought all his wares to resell to the inland villagers. He barely made it to the warehouse on three good tires; one had just blown. He drove through the large doorway and ground the truck to a halt. After that rough jaunt through the jungle it was just about through.

Hunter went to the little room that Mack Handler used for an office. He walked in and shouted, "Mack."

Mack Handler peered up from a newspaper. "Rick," he shouted in utter surprise. He stood up and walked around the desk. He was older than Rick Hunter, as his stomach showed, and considered Rick to be one of his best friends (and business associates). "What are you doing back so early? You didn't sell out yet, did you?" Mack Handler was one hundred per cent American.

"No. But I want to sell out now."

"What do you mean by that?" asked Mack, again in surprise.

"Just what I said. I'm clearing out and getting as far away from here as my money will take me."

"But why? You have such a lucrative business. You're the only link between civilization and some of the small villages."

"That's right. But there aren't any more small villages. There's a plague sweeping the jungle, killing everything. I saw one whole village completely wiped out," (He snapped his fingers) "just like that."

"Sounds bad." retorted Mack.

"It's worse than you think. Right now the plague is localized, but it's spreading like wildfire. I've already had the proper authorities notified, but I'm afraid they don't understand the severity of the matter." He paused for a minute, perhaps expecting something from Mack Handler. When he said nothing, Rick continued. "I'm going to take the next ship out of here, and I advise you to do the same."

"But Rick, I can't leave my business. Anyway, I'm expecting a new shipment today and I have to be on hand when it arrives."

Rick realized that nothing he could do or say would change his mind, so he gave up. "Well, just give me some money for my truck, and I'll leave."

That put Mack in an awkward situation. Although he had no use for the truck, he took out a bundle of bills and handed it over to Rick.

"Are you sure you won't come with me?" asked Rick.

"I think you're making a great mistake," said Mack.

"You're the one who's making the mistake, Mack." He left Mack in a state of amazement.

He walked fast down to the dock, which was not far away. But in all his haste he had to wait a half hour for the next steamer. Restlessly he sat on a bench, shaded by a straw parasol, drinking a glass of refreshingly cool lemonade. So nervous was he that he only drank half of it before it became too hot. The waiting was unbearable. He sat, got up and walked around, and sat again.

Then finally, when the steamer did come around the bend, it was slowed down by a mass of dead fish which covered the entire river. The steamer got to port, but one paddle was so fouled up that the dead fish had to be scooped out. Meanwhile a makeshift screen was rigged and placed over the front of the paddles in order to keep out the hordes of dead fish, and stop them from clogging the paddles again.

The captain, an Englishman, ran about vituperating wildly at the mess that the dead fish had made. So angry was everyone that they hardly noticed the condition of the fish. But Rick Handler scrutinized them carefully and noticed that they were wrinkled.

Rick climbed aboard and handed his ticked to the captain. He was going only as far as San Felix, since from there the steamer bore west along the Orinoco River to places such as Soledad, Las Bonitas, La Urbana, and then south as the river veered and headed for San Fernando, which was close to the Amazon and dangerously near the place where the plague would be. Instead Rick must get off at San Felix and board an ocean liner going east along the Orinoco, into the ocean and north to Trinidad. There, Rick would book passage out of the country.

The great foghorn brought Rick back to the present. The steamer was on its way at last. It slipped away from the wharf and slowly started out toward the center of the Paragua River.

There was a shout from the dock. A voice shouted, "Wait! Wait! Wait for me!" Several people moved aside to let the screeching maniac by. Rick looked toward shore and saw Mack Handler, with a small valise in his hand, running at top speed. By the time he reached the end of the pier, the steamer was about five feet away. Without halting his forward momentum he leaped through the air over the expanse of water and landed on the boat. Rick caught him and stopped him from running into the wall.

Another voice ran up the pier, shouting, "Senor, senor, you have not paid your fare." Mack extracted some coins from his pocket and threw them at the man. There was more than enough money to pay for the ride.

For the first time Rick Hunter had time to say something. "Mack, I'm sure glad you're here. But what made you change your mind?"

Mack wiped perspiration off his face and said, "A radio announcement came from San Rafael. They said they got a weird report from San Jose. Something about a vast disease that was going right through the streets, killing plants and animals. They got across some details of people dropping dead in the streets, then the whole city went dead. Not a word has come from it since. Down in San Rafael they're getting plenty scared.

By now probably half of Paragua has been warned to start evacuation procedures.

"That was enough for me, what with you storming in and leaving. And you had been in the jungle. I just gathered up some valuables, locked up the warehouse, and ran down here as fast as I could. You'd been gone so long that I felt sure you had already left.

"It's because of the Nothing that the steamer was late in leaving." Rick smiled.

"The Nothing . . . " stammered Mack.

"Just a name I made up for it. Come over here and look." Rick drew Mack to the side of the boat and pointed in the water at the dead fish. Mack whistled in astonishment, or perhaps fear.

Rich took Mack to a secluded corner of the ship and sat down at a table. "This is real bad, Mack. There's never been anything like it before. To tell you the truth, I'm scared."

"You're not alone in that," Mack reassured him.

"I don't understand what this Nothing is, but I heard some reports of the villagers. And I was there when it started moving through the jungle. It kills everything. I saw a line as far as I could see in either direction coming after me, killing everything in its path. Trees went down like nothing. And the condition it leaves its victims in . . . " He described as close as possible Francisco's description of Pedro.

By this time the steamer had beat its way ahead of the dead fish. Now they were in the clear and picking up time. Soon they passed Curucay and an hour later passed from the Paragua River to the Caroni River. Less than a hundred miles separated them from San Felix.

Since Rick had several hours until the steamer reached port, he procured some paper and a pen and set down to write everything he knew about the Nothing. When he had finished, San Felix was just around the bend, on the great Orinoco River. He stuffed the paper inside his dusty and sweaty shirt.

Before the steamer even touched dock, the two men had disembarked. They went straight to the ticket office and inquired about ships going east. They were in luck, for a small liner was in dock now and was leaving for Trinidad in ten minutes. They bought the tickets and found the boat. They were each assigned a cabin, where they could sleep on the long overnight voyage. After that they would go . . . Where? When Rick thought it over he concluded that he would welcome passage anywhere north.

Rick got some much-needed sleep, and Mack forced himself to lie down until he finally dozed off. Meanwhile, on its way to Port of Spain, Trinidad, the ship made two stops. First it stopped at Nuima Island, at the mouth of the Orinoco River where the vast ocean lay ahead. Then, for a swift exchange of passengers, it stopped at the most southern point of Trinidad, Galeota Point. From there it rounded Icacos Point, in the middle of the Gulf of Paria. Both men were oblivious to this.

Mack Handler awoke and saw that just a half hour separated the ship from port. He got up, went next door to Rick's cabin, and roused him out of a fitful sleep.

"Come on, Rick. We'd better eat something before we leave for shore. Only a half hour left if we're on time.

Rick got up dazedly from his comatose stupor and shakily went on deck to eat. They had a good meal of hot pancakes and coffee and were ready for their departure.

It was a refreshing idea to be away from the jungle, and the city looked bright and gay from the sea. Eagerly the two men sought to be ashore. The great ship pulled up to dock and Rick and Mack waited impatiently while the ramp was lowered. As soon as it was in place they ran down. But they had only gotten halfway when an armed patrol squealed up to the dock and a task force of a dozen strong men equipped with rifles emerged. Rick got the impression that he was not wanted on shore.

As they backed up the gangplank, the spokesman took out an amplifier and shouted: "We have gotten word from the mainland of a great plague. I must tell you that you must remain aboard until further notice, since we do not wish to spread contagion. Please make yourselves at home. That is all."

The speech was curt and to the point. But it did not end there. The captain was furious. He ran down the gangplank screaming bloody murder. (Another Englishman!) However, after several shots ricocheted off the wooden ramp he turned and ran up the plank in double time. That did not stop the argument, though. From his ship he argued down at the dock. The military man held his decor and temper. When the captain brought out the fact that he had already dropped passengers off at Galeota Point, it came over the loudspeaker that they had been rounded up and placed under quarantine.

The fight raged on, but Rick and Mack retreated to their stateroom to discuss the situation.

"Mack, we have to get off this boat. I know the Nothing is not contagious, but I can't tell them that," Rick said thoughtfully.

"I think the captain is so riled up he'd probably give us a lifeboat just to be in defiance of them."

Rick considered that aspect for a moment, then spoke out. "That's it! If we can find an inflatable rubber life raft, we can row our way out of here. But to get overboard without anyone seeing us will be the only problem."

They both agreed on that plan of action. The fault was that they could only leave under the protection of darkness. So for the daylight hours they surveyed the ship and figured their course. They stole a life raft and oars and kept them in Mack's cabin. Then they waited.

Meanwhile, the captain was still arguing. First he said that he would submit to a complete medical examination. When that was refused he attempted to untie the mooring ropes and head back for the mainland. But a few whizzing bullets soon put that thought out of mind. They would not let him come ashore, yet they would not let him leave.

When nightfall finally did come, the two men were ready to leave. They were surveying the soldiers through the porthole. Rick opened it without attracting unwanted attention. Then they gathered sheets and pillows from Mack's cabin and put it in Rick's, together with his flammable objects. They ignited the great pile of cloth and then ran out of the room. Mack had the raft inside his shirt, thus increasing his apparent obesity. The two short oars Mack held up his sleeves. They casually went on deck until the fire was noticed. Then, when everyone's attention was focused on that area, they made good their escape.

Mack took the raft out from under his shirt and while he fumbled with the oars, Rick inflated it by pulling the plug of the carbon dioxide canister. He threw the raft overboard and jumped in. Then he helped Mack down and together they rowed away. At first they went straight out so as to get away from the ship's lights. Then they cut around and headed for shore.

They beached the raft and ran along the shore until they reached a boat rental service. They offered a large amount of money, but the reply was bleakly:

"I would like to, but the police have ordered that no boats may leave on any pretense."

So they did the next best thing. They knocked him out and tied him up. Then they looked over the boats and settled for a nice twenty-footer. They took off and for about five miles hugged the shore. They went out around the peninsula, twice avoiding patrol boats, and landed near a boat drive-in. Then they stocked up on food and water and left a handsome tip to the friendly proprietor.

They steered into the wide Caribbean Sea, in a north-northwesterly direction at top speed. They had planned on taking the Mona Passage (between the island of the Dominican Republic and Haiti, and the island of Puerto Rico), along the Bahamas and to Florida. But they miscalculated the propinquity of the Nothing. It swept silently across the sea, giving no warning of its coming. It killed every living creature in the sea or in the air above it. It even drew the life from floating pollen and seeds. Rick Hunter and Mack Handler never knew it when the Nothing got them.

*   *   *   *   *

Tom Parley sat in his laboratory reading the newspaper, while his two assistants, Sam Clemmet and Edward J. Kirsly, were bent over long strings of data sheets. The room was in utter silence, except for the labored breathing of the head scientist. Finally he rose from his comfortable lounging chair and threw the paper down on it. Big headlines stared up in bold letters:

NOTHINGOSIS ATTACKS SOUTH AMERICA
Diary Found on Victim
Scientists Scorn in Disbelief

"It's amazing," said Sam Clemmet. "Absolutely amazing. I've never seen anything like it. Here, take a look at it, Ed."

Ed Kirsly read the cosmic radiation sheet like a printed page. To anyone unfamiliar with the machine, such a thing would look like a compilation of jagged lines. But its meaning was very real (or unreal) to the young scientist.

"It's odd," stammered Kirsly. "As a matter of fact, it's impossible."

"But why did you wait until now to tell us this?" asked Clemmet.

"I don't really know. Perhaps I was afraid of scorn. But I really thought that there was something wrong with the machine, which is why I had it checked over completely before allowing myself any deduction. I had to have time to think over this thing first. Besides, a scientist has a right to keep a new discovery to himself for a little while."

"Yes, but certainly not three days." That was Clemmet.

"Anyone would be hesitant about something like that. But now, new evidence has come to light, and I think I've got the answer.

"About the anti-radiation pocket you mean?"

"Of course. Here, let me show you the newspaper. I suppose you've already seen it, but perhaps you didn't notice the correlation." Parley laid the paper on his desk next to data sheets. Then he placed them in a certain way and picked them up together, taking them to the large map screen. "Now look at this. The anti-radiation pocket followed this course through Venezuela." He traced his finger along the map. "And I lost contact of it just about here. Now look at this map in the newspaper. So far the so-called nothingosis has covered almost all of Venezuela, and parts of surrounding countries. And the farthest extent of it is a perfect circle, of which the hub is right here in Venezuela, which is just past where I lost contact of the anti-radiation pocket. There is a definite correlation."

"Yes. And the diary of that fellow Hunter tells about a huge meteorite which followed that path. And he states that the plague started just after that."

Kirsly was just catching up.

"Precisely. So there must be a connection there," said Clemmet.

"All right, now before you get to far ahead, I'd better tell you the whole gruesome story. You may not like it, but I'm afraid that what I have to say is so exactingly true that the severity of the situation at hand is immediate." Parley was now serious. It made Clemmet and Kirsly shudder.

"Here's the way it is, fact and theory. A meteorite landed in South America. In the same path my cosmic ray detector followed something which I classify as anti-radiation, for lack of better nomenclature. No, wait a moment, let me call it a radiation shield. The meteorite is made out of something not which repels cosmic radiation, but simply shields from it."

"Now, in the precise place where this meteorite landed, a plague begins: a plague which is so vast, so omnipresent that it takes the life of every living thing it touches. For simplicity's sake, I will call this plague the Nothing, since that word best fits all the facts. The

Nothing is not a plague, but an alien life form so different from ours that it is practically inconceivable.

"Perhaps it is more advanced than Man, I do not know, but there is no reason to suppose that Man is the end of evolution. On the contrary, I believe that evolution has no end. Soon, perhaps, with the withering away of the body, evolution will carry life into pure energy, of which I believe the Nothing to be a form. But energy cannot reproduce itself. But wait, I'm getting ahead of myself.

"The Nothing is a living organism - no a living entity. But energy cannot live. There can be no such thing as living energy. Therefore, the only deduction is that the Nothing is a form of parasitic energy. It has no life of its own, so it is forced to take life from real living organisms.

"There is something which keeps us alive. Freud called it the libido, the energy of all life instincts. Every living organism had this libido, no matter how simple or complex. When we eat we are eating the libido of other organisms, and thus we are kept alive. When we die the libido departs, most at the instant of death, the rest fades away slowly until the matter of the body is absorbed.

"But we are dealing here with a life form that is not a physical organism. Thus it can contain no libido, since it will slowly slip away. So the Nothing has turned parasite. Since it is constantly losing libidos, it must replenish its supply with fresh ones. Result: when the libido is suddenly drawn out of an organism, that organism dies."

They were stunned. Kirsly sat still and quiet, pondering the matter. But Clemmet pulled himself out of his daze and offered further theory to the matter. "Well, if all life must have a libido to live and reproduce, then technically the Nothing is dead."

"I hadn't really thought of that before, but I suppose that you are right. The Nothing is - dead. But as long as it retains the capacity to take life wills from real, living organisms, it can sustain its existence. That's it.

The Nothing doesn't live, it exists."

Kirsly had been watching the conversation pretty closely, but had not said anything. Apparently he was not sold on the idea. "It seems to me that you are taking this pretty lightly, Sam."

"I'm inclined to believe it. And one thing in his favor is this: can you offer anything better?"

"No, I can't. But I would like to know how you happened to come about to formulate such a wild, outrageous idea, Tom." Kirsly directed his gaze at the older scientist.

For answer Parley strode back to his desk and extracted several newspapers from a drawer. "There are scanty reports of theories of eminent scientists from all over the world. Some are propagated by crackpots, but others have a very good background. I had the beginning of a theory in my mind, and I read the theories of others to complete mine. It is astonishing to note the similarity between my theories and some others. By the way, there is one more thing I haven't yet told you."

Parley thumbed through the newspapers. "Here it is." After he located the proper page he began another phase of his theory.

"Look at this map. It shows the entire world on scale, with Venezuela at its hub, at precisely the same place where the Nothing began. It is now positively known that the Nothing works on cycles. From Rick Hunters diary (he's the man they found afloat in the Gulf Stream) and from known scientific observations they have plotted the extent of the Nothing. So far the Nothing has gone through four cycles and is now in a latency period. Let me explain the significance of those terms. The Nothing is cyclic in movement. It has a sudden surging forth, during which it is in it's "eating" period. During that it takes libidos out of every living thing it touches, using the energy it took on the cycle before. Then, when it runs out of energy it stops the advancement and draws back. It retreats slightly to digest the newly captured libidos, called the latency period, then it advances again. Each advance is geometrically proportioned to the preceding, with the effect that the bigger it gets, the bigger it will become."

"Right now it has just passed the fourth expansion period, and is resting. In the next period it will encompass a good portion of the islands in the Caribbean Sea. During the seventh it will take over just about all of Florida. Then we are next. Florida has over four days left. We have under six."

"And this is absolute fact?" asked Clemmet.

"Absolute, scientific fact." said Parley. Then he turned to Kirsly and asked, "What do you think?"

"I think that . . . No, I don't know what to think."

"You still don't believe me?" asked Parley, stunned. "Well, someone was right when he said that sagacity matures with age."

"Just remember that senility also matures with age." offered Kirsly, angry at his age inferiority.

"I'm sorry," apologized Parley. " But let's not get into an argument."

"All right. But now that you've told us your apology, what are you going to do?"

Parley put his head down, as if in embarrassment. "This part comes especially hard for me. But first I have to explain something else. Obviously a theory is nothing unless we can back it up with proofs. But the only proof we need will answer another question, also. We know that when the Nothing came to earth, it was encased in a shell which is impervious to radiation. The only possible reason for this is that cosmic radiation is harmful - perhaps deadly - to it. Here, on a planet whose atmosphere shields its inhabitants from most of the radiation from space, it has discarded its shell so that it might live again. Here it is safe from the effects which radiation may have on it."

"If, as my theory states, the Nothing is pure energy, then cosmic radiation, which is nothing more than super-speeded energy, will probably overcome it, or nullify it. There is our goal. We must create a machine which can somehow intensify the radiation which naturally reaches us through our veil of atmosphere."

"We can't intensify cosmic radiation, Tom." said Clemmet.

"No, that was a poor choice of words, I admit."

"But wait a minute." Sudden inspiration came to Clemmet. "How about that photon energizer we almost have completed. If we can work out all the bugs and make a unit big enough, we can use a beam of light to . . . to conquer, or at least deter, the Nothing as an entity."

Kirsly again entered the conversation. "I haven't yet assented to the reality of the Nothing as an entity?"

"What?" shouted Parley and Clemmet in unison.

"However, I'm willing to cooperate. I still work for you, Tom. And I still have high admiration for your intelligence. I will do anything you ask, but when you actually prove that there is a Nothing, then, and only then, will I consent to having possessed the knowledge from this conversation."

"Well, I guess I'll have to take you up on that. But for now, let's get to work."

*   *   *   *   *

The undertaking of such a task was an immense responsibility. But the deciding factor was the less than six days in which they had to put he entire apparatus together. However, with eighty-seven highly trained scientists and technicians working on the project, there was a very good chance that it might be finished and put into operating condition before he deadline (literally).

A suggestion had been made to transfer all the necessary materials to Indonesia, which was diametrically antipodal to Venezuela, but there was too much to settle in too short a time. And besides that, such confusion raged over the world that transportation was non-existent as far as civilians with crazy Messiah thoughts were concerned. No, humanity's last stand would take place in Texas. Perhaps.

The photon energizer, on which they had been working for some time, had been limited to the amount of money allotted it, for with unlimited expenses it could run into a great deal of money. Now that the need for the instrument was imminent, all the money at Parley's hands went into it. It had been completed on small scale, with just about perfect functions. Now, those imperfections would be ironed out and it would - or might be - ready for use against the Nothing.

A great long list of needed equipment was drawn up and a dozen men were delegated to pick it up at any expense. Although much of the supplies could be gotten from nearby Dallas, some of the more intricate and unusual instruments were manufactured by only one company in the far away corner of the state, or even out of state. And the most important part (although every part was almost as important as any other) was ordered from Miami Beach, Florida, from which it was to be flown out.

There were never less than one hundred carpenters working at any hour. They were busy building the many closet-sized houses around the outer periphery of the hill on which the labs were set. This was to be the wall of defense against the Nothing. They were also installing two new buildings and sectioning them off into small rooms for the many people who would have to be housed.

Complications arose, naturally, but they were usually resolved in the most expensive manner. The saying that traversed the "Family" grapevine was, "We'll take it anyway, and figure out what to do with it later." Many things, about which there was some doubt, had to be dispersed with without delay. For instance, the female secretaries were sent into town to buy necessities for the project. They came back with truckloads of articles which men would never have thought of but which were, in fact, given the name "necessities." This also included scores of plumbers to build bathrooms for the entire populace of Project Nothing. The labs were already self-sufficient in that they had their own wells and water supply and electricity.

By the time carpentry had been done, all sorts of animals arrived to fill up the space that had been left for various forms of livestock. There was one room partitioned off especially for animals. Among other useful animals were caged cattle, sheep, chickens, several forms of functional birds, many kinds of insects, and man's best friend, the dog (in three breeds). All in all it looked like a Noah's Ark.

The plant room was replete with vegetable and fruit seeds. Some were allowed to grow for food, but they took up much less space in embryonic form. There were very few flowers, since they were not essential for human life. All the grains were represented, also.

But the most important - and most heartless - was the incorporation of human females. And this was the first thing that had come to Tom Parley's mind when he thought of undertaking such a task.

The way in which he went about it was quite simple . He advertised all over Dallas for intelligent, scientifically trained women between the ages of twenty-one and thirty (the most fertile period in the female cycle) and offered exorbitant wages and good conditions with light work (and indeed the former and latter were entirely true). Many applicants were fighting, vying for the job, but since five hundred were wanted, the only ones turned down were the physically unfit. They did not have the time to give psychological tests, fertility tests, and a hundred other complex tests for survival, only because of the time limit.

The girls were set straight when they went into the Dallas office. They were told that there was no pay whatsoever, the conditions would be cramped and horrible, and their sole function was for the chronic propagation of the human race. None refused.

Near the end of four days, applicants dropped off suddenly, because of evacuation, so to reach their quota they had to take some of the poorer specimens. But when all was told, including the wives of some of the scientists working for Tom Parley, the amount totaled five hundred forty females, as contrasted with the ninety males on Project Nothing. Not a word more be said.

Needless to say, the major problem, what with all these six hundred thirty people and all the animals, was food. Most of the animals had to have their regular diet, but man was going to subsist on a diet of concentrates and vitamins. They were drab and tasteless, but space saving. The function was not to be palatable as much as to be nourishing.

All in all, with the many scientists working on the photon energizer and the many women thinking up and buying all sorts of things vital to the success of the project, everything would be finished by the deadline except for one thing. The vacuum tube ordered from Florida was not going to be delivered by air as specified - or by any other method. Because of immediate evacuation movements taking place in Florida, the entire company had left the state, with the completed tube having been left behind, in the warehouse. A telegram came to Tom Parley, saying shortly and curtly where it was to be found if they still wanted it. Parley could do nothing but go after it. And he had less than twenty-four hours in which to get it.

*   *   *   *   *

Tom Parley and Sam Clemmet boarded the former's private Piper Cub at the Dallas airport and readied the vehicle for its flight to Florida. Ed Kirsly had been left behind to take charge of Project Nothing. They had stored in the plane four guinea pigs and electroencephalographic equipment. Their purpose was to find the exact time the Nothing touched Florida and thus be able to figure precisely at what time it would hit Dallas. Also stored was ample fuel to get them back, since they were not expecting Miami to be any too receptive. Parley doubted that there was any airplane fuel left in Miami, and the project was too important to be halted by a lack of foresight.

Miami was less than eight hundred miles, so that it would take just about eight hours to reach it. They made the flight in very good time, and landed without incident. Parley taxied the plane into a massive hangar and turned it around. The two men took out their equipment and once outside the hangar, closed the massive doors. He just had to hope that no one would find it. As he looked around the airport he did not see one plane anywhere. They had all left for the north a long time ago.

The only vehicle they found was a handcart, on which they loaded their equipment and the guinea pigs. This they wheeled out of the airport and to the street. There it was like a madhouse. Cars were jammed tight because of a stalled car farther along the road. But no time was wasted in pushing it off the road, despite fiery protests from the driver. Then traffic speeded up somewhat. There was a constant honking of horns and always total confusion. Somehow they had to get to the address where the precious vacuum tube was stored. Tom Parley was getting desperate. He had not expected such animalism from human beings, and his genetic pride was hurt considerably by what he saw.

The two were almost run down twice, in their attempt to flag down a car or enter through the door of a stalled automobile. But it was understandable why the people were so frightened, since only ten hours remained.

Finally, however, one truck pulled into a gasoline station about a half a block away. He was pumping some gasoline for himself, since the attendants had long since departed. Parley and Clemmet approached him warily.

"Stay back," shouted the obviously scared man. "Stay back or I'll shoot." He deftly displayed a shining black pistol and thumbed the hammer.

"But we only want to use your truck for a while." Parley answered. He knew it sounded silly, but he said it anyway.

"Nobody uses this truck but me." That was final.

The pressure was rising now. If they did not accomplish their aim soon, they might get caught up the seething maelstrom of humanity. And they could not die because of the meddling of an ignorant layman. After all, they were scientists.

"But, listen. I've got to get to . . . " he read off the address from the telegram which he had just taken out of his pocket.

"That's about two miles north of here, just off this road. I'll tell you how to get there, but that's all." He finished pumping gasoline into his truck; either that or the pump was empty.

"I'll tell you what. I've got an airplane locked up in the airport. If you'll drive us there and back, I'll fly you out of here."

"A likely story," replied the sinister man, while his face bent into an odd contortion and his thick dark mustache bent up in a sneer.

"Well, the least you can do is let us hop a ride to the place, if you're going right by the place." Sam Clemmet spoke up for the first time.

The man pondered this for a couple seconds, then agreed. "All right, get in. But I'm warning you now, you better not try any funny stuff."

Eagerly they piled their equipment into the back of the truck and climbed in. The truck forced its way into the long line of cars and rumbled along slowly. It took them a half hour to go the two miles.

"Hey, you two. We're here. Get out."

While Clemmet took out all the instruments, Parley tried to sweet talk the man. "Mister, I'm not kidding about the plane. We'll only be about a half hour and then we have to get back to the airport. If you help us we can get you out of here ten times faster than you can on the ground."

He hesitated. Then: "Well, I guess you got a point there. But getting back is going to be tough."

"Thanks. Thanks a lot, Mister."

Together Parley and Clemmet loaded the truck again. Then the driver veered off along a side road and in two more minutes arrived at the specified address.

"This is it." He shouted. It was not a very impressive place. It was fairly large, but run down beyond repair. They unloaded the equipment and set it down in front of the door. The big driver punched in a windowpane and crawled into the building. He found his way to the door and unlocked it for the two scientists. They ran in and set down the equipment.

"Let's find the vacuum tube first. It's about four feet long and a foot and a half wide." They went into the storeroom and saw that there were many boxes of various sizes lying around. They were all scientific instruments, although some pertained to other fields of research. The driver found a large box which had the words "vacuum tube" printed on the side, along with "handle with extreme care." They opened it up carefully, just to make sure it was the right one. It was, so they dragged it out into the first room.

Then they started to set up the electroencephalograph. Parley hooked up the instruments while Clemmet Attached the radio sender to the animals. This would transmit the brain waves to Dallas where they would be picked up, even before they would get back to see it.

The two men worked fast, but still the truck driver was impatient. He paced up and down, saying: "Aren't you finished with that thing yet? Traffic's getting worse every minute."

When it was completed, the driver uttered something to the effect of, "It's about time." Hurriedly the three men lifted the vacuum tube onto the truck. It had been packed with infinite care and half the weight of the box was in newspaper. Clemmet stayed in the back of the truck so that he could keep an eye on the box and steady it.

The big truck driver wasted no time in racing the truck out of there, but when he reached the highway he found that traffic was so bad that there was not even enough room walk. There were no courteous drivers to let them through, either.

"I know another back road to the airport, but it's mighty bumpy." said the truck driver.

"We'll have to chance it," said Parley, shaking his head woefully.

The truck driver wheeled the truck around and

went back the way he had just come. He passed the warehouse again and went on for about half a mile. There he took an intersecting street which went parallel to the main highway. To say that the road was a might bumpy was a gross understatement, for potholes the size of bathtubs studded the street. The truck did a very good job of skirting these, and all in all made better time than they did on the crowded highway.

The truck rounded the edge of the airport where the highway was located. He steered the truck along the choked highway in the drainage ditch. The truck tilted on a great angle, but not enough to tip over. Then he pulled it out and into the gate. Parley directed him to the proper hanger. When they reached it, Clemmet jumped out of the truck and opened the two massive doors. Then he jumped into the truck as it went by.

The driver parked the truck alongside the airplane. The three men together lifted the tube up and stacked it in the storage compartment. While Clemmet secured it, Parley took out the extra fuel and refilled the tank. As the gasoline went into the tank, Parley handed the hose to the truck driver. Then he walked to the side of the hangar and picked up a heavy monkey wrench.

The truck driver looked inside the tank and when he saw that it was empty said, "Its all in. Now maybe we can get out . . . " He never finished the sentence, for Tom Parley had conked him over the head with the monkey wrench. He was quite dead.

"What . . . what did you do that for?" stammered Clemmet. He could not have been more stunned, more petrified.

"I had to do it. If we had taken him back with us, he would want to come with us to the lab. And if we refused he would have let out the secret of what we are doing. He wouldn't have fit into our plans. He is psychologically, socially, and mentally not in accordance with our team at the Hill. I want the best possible human beings to continue the race. He was too radically different. So I had to dispose of him."

Parley threw down the monkey wrench and boarded the plane. Clemmet just stood there with his mouth open. He just could not believe that Parley would do a thing like that. Parley started the motors and slowly Clemmet got in.

He taxied the little Piper Cub out onto the field, glanced at the weather vane, and went down the proper runway according to the wind direction.

Misfortune was really after Parley that day, for at the far end of the field three indistinct shapes were running toward the airplane. Parley poured on all the speed he could get out of the plane, but it was not enough. The three people were running so fast, and the plane would not rise quickly enough. There was a thump as the landing gear smashed into them.

The collision jolted the airplane more that it disturbed its pilot. It veered down and bounced on the runway. Then, as it went into the air, Parley yanked back on the wheel. The plane rose, but not quite enough. It cleared the fence, only to run into a grove of palm trees beyond. Since the forward momentum was greater and the give in the trees was less, the landing gear immediately snapped off, hardly shaking the airplane.

Slowly he brought the plane up, and at the same time it veered off toward the west and headed for Texas. Parley pushed the plane to the limit of its speed capabilities, for he was anxious to get away from that place of horror and insanity. He had never seen such animosity among fellow human beings. But so much for those silly ignorant people, he thought. He was a scientist, and he would not be diverted from his course - his goal. The supremacy of man was imminent, and Parley was the first of a new breed.

He was in for a rough landing at Dallas.

           *   *   *   *   *

The landing was rough.

Because of spontaneous evacuation movements the airport was just about deserted. There were few attendants, but all airworthy craft had already taken off and none were expected back.

The small Piper Cub circled around the airport for about five minutes - that got rid of all the extra fuel they had. Although Parley radioed the tower that he had no landing gear, there was nothing whatsoever they could do about it. So, he was forced to attempt a crash landing. He picked out the smoothest grass plot he could find in the short space of time allotted to him and set the plane down.

It bounced a couple of times, skidded, striking sparks on mislaid stones, and ground to a rasping halt not more than twenty feet from the cemented runway. Needless to say, the airplane would never fly again, mostly because the bottom had been scraped off until grass stuck up through the floor into the pilot's compartment.

Most important, the giant vacuum tube was all right. It had been secured tightly and thus suffered no damaging jolts. Many vehicles rushed up to the airplane, including Tom Parley's own truck, which was to transport the vacuum tube. The crowd dispersed almost immediately when they saw that no one was hurt.

The transfer of the vacuum tube was done quickly and efficiently, but with extreme care. It was bedded down in the straw, so that the shock of the bumpy road would not seem as hard. The truck went slowly, and after a half hour had only reached the base of the hill. The ascent was gradual, and slow, and it took another fifteen minutes to get to the top.

There was some rejoicing when the truck ambled into the confines of the laboratories. Parley hushed it down and refrained from a speech because of the presence of the workers.

He was quite surprised at the number of females he saw. They were everywhere and got into everything. They ran around doing errands, or some form of light work. They were all fine specimens, both physically and mentally. But the most surprising part was that they seemed happy. Parley had not dared to hope such a response. Then, when he actually thought about it, it did not seem so unreal. After all, was not the purpose of every woman to bear children; and did not most women feel this as an essential part of life? Perhaps they were glad at the idea that they were the most important facet of the project, and having children, which many wished to do anyway, was their ticket to such a feeling of want, instead of need.

Parley made his way to his own part of the laboratory. It was next to the room which held the center of power for the photon energizer. Many people were so glad to see him back that they shook his hand vigorously. What has happened to the temperament of these people, thought Parley? He did not know what had made everyone so "glad to be alive," but he himself felt the same way. It was a good feeling.

The time for the attack neared. The exact time, give or take two minutes, had been computed from the government report, so that they knew when the deadline was. The men watching the electroencephalograph had measured the distance between the warehouse and where the last line was, clocked how long it took the Nothing to reach that point, and thus figured out its speed.

The radius of the Nothing's advancement was now approximately two thousand five hundred miles. When it finished its next advancement it would be about four thousand miles.

Tension mounted as the end neared; mostly it started in the laborers and was transferred to the rest of the men and women. As a result, they let all the workers go a full day ahead of time. They received generous helpings of worthless green paper, and seemed pleased to get it. The small amount of work that remained was pretty easy, and Parley thought that everyone together could finish it in a very few days.

The final hour came. The five hundred forty women, ninety men, and the few children stood outside in the beautiful sunlight, gazing toward the southeast. They stood on the ground, steadied themselves on chairs, and covered the five roofs.

Anxiety arose when the machine was turned on, for anyone in the beam of the photon energizer would suffer severe radiation burns and chance genetic mutation. But inside the sphere all was well. Hands were gripped tightly as the motors warmed up. It came by word of mouth that it was functioning properly, since the machine noise could only be heard inside the main lab.

There was a little rejoicing then, but it faded away quickly. Then, on the horizon, visible only in binoculars, trees seemed to fall. The line of death was racing madly across the plain toward them.

It happened very fast. The uneasy men and women watched the grass outside the sphere of radiation. They knew what to expect. Suddenly the grass turned a sickening shade of brown; bushes were seen to wrinkle; and trees fell with a deadening thud.

Then, before they could realize the horror of it, the Nothing had passed. All around the Hill was death: three hundred sixty degrees of Nothing. No life existed beyond the Hill, as far as its inhabitants were concerned: not in the air, on the land, or under the sea. Death was everywhere. But there was a feeling, an omnipresence of something - of nothing.

They had safely defied the Nothing.

Now they had to defeat it.

*   *   *   *   *

After two months of confinement the team was getting edgy.

The feeling of supremacy had worn off and the feeling of loneliness had set in. The Nothing had finished its outward surge thirty days before, after killing every living organism except the gods of the Hill. The only thing that kept them alive was the photon energizer and patience. The latter was failing.

The community was getting along terribly because of previous marital differences. Women were constantly vying for the comparatively few men. The proportion of women over men was six to one.

From the male's standpoint of view, it turned out to

be worse than they had expected. Having first had the impression that general promiscuity was going to be fun, they soon learned that they could not satisfy all the females. There was always some alluring woman tempting a man. And for married men this was indeed a problem.

Parley had tried to explain that there was no cause for jealousy. But on one would listen. In fact, he even made matters worse. He was soon scoffed off as a crackpot scientist who had only extended for a short while the misery of their lives.

There was constant bickering among the females. Several times they had broken into bloody fights. The women soon found that by sheer force of numbers they were reduced in status from the men. And those who had been successfully impregnated were more reduced because they were discarded like used and unwanted articles. With these and many other problems Parley found himself the hub of a rotating wheel of restraint.

Propinquity made it even worse. Everywhere one turned there were people. People occupied every crack and corner, nook and cranny. Sometimes people felt the need to go somewhere distant from the constant humming of civilization - away from people. Because inwardly, people hated people.

Parley knew that the only way to stop them from thinking about each other was to dissuade their minds. He tried to create work. But in such a small area with so many people he simply could not find enough work to be done. Sure, the men were always trying to expand the sphere of influence of the photon energizer, but every attempt had failed. People were going mad.

All in all, it was not working out as Parley had planned. He had gone on the supposition that intelligence would overcome animalistic inhibitions. But as it turned out it was more of a hindrance, for they fretted over their inability to fight the Nothing. Parley was irritated by the incompetence of his men to cope with reality and take the Nothing in stride. His attitude toward the women changed too. They no longer remained passive, living their lives with the sole intention of propagating it. They had come alive to the fact that they were being treated like slaves.

Tom Parley's intentions were wholly altruistic. He had undertaken this immense task with the full understanding that individuals did not count - it was the continuation of the race that was important. And when - he never said it in his thoughts - he conquered the Nothing he would breed his new kind of man. Not just man, but a super being that would care about life; a super being that would look out for his inferiors. Man must rule the universe - of that he was certain.

Perhaps he was wrong in his anthropomorphism of man. Perhaps man was not meant be ubiquitous and omniscient. Meant! That was a meaningless word. Nothing was meant to be. One must make it for himself. Parley could not bring himself to believe in the foreordainment of life, because that led to inevitability, which in turn was an impossibility. Nature took its course, but Man changed his. Man had become ultranatural - or was it extranatural?

Parley's philosophical train of though was broken by Ed Kirsly's enraged voice. He stormed through the door, trailed by his pleading wife. Kirsly was one of the more critical cases, in need of treatment by a good psychiatrist. Of course, Parley had never thought of bringing one of such an occupation into his establishment. This was an unforeseen event of equally unforeseen consequences.

"Ed, I love you," cried Kirsly's wife, Jane.

"Don't you understand that there is no room for love anymore?" shouted Kirsly.

He grabbed her shoulders and shook her violently.

"What is going on here," said Parley, barely making his voice audible over Jane's weeping.

"I'm trying to make her understand that marriage is no longer a cherished item. It's passé. It's obsolete."

"Ed, you can't mean that . . . "

"I can and do mean every word of it. Anyway, why should my whole life revolve around *you*. I've got my choice of hundreds of others. What makes you think that I *belong* to you . . . ?

He would have said more but Jane slapped him hard across the face. "Why, you little . . . "

"Grab hold of yourself," shouted Parley.

For an answer he got a fist under his eye. Jane turned and ran toward the door.

"Oh, no you don't," said Kirsly.

He grabbed her and swung her around facing him. He was probably going to do something to her, but just then the door burst open and several angry faces glared at Kirsly. They paused for a moment, then charged him. Kirsly threw his wife at them and ran toward the massive machinery that was the main body of the photon energizer. They ran after the obviously insane man, but he climbed the side of the machine and perched on a ledge. The machinery was thirty feet long, ten feet wide and the top was fifteen feet from the ground. This was the enormous energy drawer which motivated the photon energizer. And a madman was loose on it. But was he mad enough to betray the entire human race?

By now there were about fifty people crowded in the room. Parley did not know what Kirsly had done that was so terrible. Perhaps it was a small thing that had been psychologically built into a monstrous misdemeanor. But he knew that he had to calm down not only Kirsly but the mob as well. However, he never had a chance.

"I say we rush him, now. He can't do anything," came a voice from the crowd.

"He's mad," shouted another.

"Get him away from there before he kills us all," a woman spoke.

"Wait!" yelled Tom Parley. By that word he had hoped to avert the attention of the crowd so that he could try to appease them. But, instinctually, Kirsly's head jerked around and faced the speaker. At the same time two men leaped up the massive machinery. One got his face kicked in, the other grabbed Kirsly's foot and hung on, shouting.

"Get him. Get him . . . "

The crowd surged forward and Kirsly, fighting for his life, wrenched his foot free and slithered up the machine toward the one vulnerable part - the vacuum tube. If he broke that, all was lost.

Gasping, Kirsly ran up the side of the huge mechanism. Fear mounted in him, because he had his back turned on the mob. He was weak, and his legs shook. As he mounted the railing which indicated the apex of the machine on which the vacuum tube lay, a pang of fear so strong raged through him that he collapsed, his legs no longer able to carry the weight of his body.

As his forward momentum impelled him, he threw his hands ahead to stop the awful collision, but his elbows buckled and his head crushed into the glass. There was a crack of glass, and a sudden implosion. Minute glass particles blasted the body of Ed Kirsly, cut it to ribbons and tossed it to the ground. Glass showered the mob, and Tom Parley suffered from several cuts.

Immediately the crowd grasped the potential of the scene they had just witnessed. They yelled, ran, and clawed for the doorway like frightened animals. They had to run, to get away, not from the glass, but from the Nothing!

But where to run, thought Tom Parley. The Nothing was everywhere. Nevertheless, Parley ran for his life. He went through the side door and into his private office. His mind was fogged, unclear. He did not know where to go, or where he was going.

He just ran blindly.

On the other side of the office was his laboratory. He raced through there, teetering unsteadily. He crashed into a rack of chemicals and it turned over, splattering unknown solutions onto the floor. Parley gathered himself up from that, and before he knew it he was in the animal room.

The smell of hay and manure reached his nostrils. He ran down the corridor, lined with cattle, sheep, and goats on one side, chickens, ducks, and rabbits on the other. He reached the intersection and, gasping for breath, held himself up by holding tenaciously onto a cage bar. He glanced behind him and saw simultaneously the cattle and chickens wither up and collapse. Then the sheep and ducks. Then . . .

Parley waited no longer. He ran down the corridor and into the plant room. He did not bother to note what kind of plants. He was half way down the length of the room when he remembered that the only other door - to the outside - lay at the end of the room from which he had already come. But it was too late to turn back. One row of plants withered, burned brown and drooped to the bottom of the earth-filled boxes.

Parley backed up slowly. Then he turned around and ran. Blindly, he smashed into the wall. He felt his way along it with sweating hands. Finally he found himself in the corner, with no place to go. He drew himself up and whimpered. Slowly, purposefully, the Nothing advanced. Rows of plants went through the process of death and lay down in the boxes, their coffins. The last row of plants suddenly drooped over, and when they were flat in their boxes, Parley cried.

"Oh. God. No-o-o-o-o . . . "

He threw his hands over his eyes and wept. It seemed like a long time that he wept, and indeed it must have been for his eyes were red and his hands salty with the film of tears.

Unknowingly he motivated his hands. They drew away from his face and he gazed across the room. There stood rows of plants, all beautiful, all alive.

Parley did not understand, *could* not understand. Dazedly he arose and walked trancelike outside. There, strewn on the ground in odd contortions, were the hundreds of bodies of his companions.

Parley stared out at the large expanse of land that was visible on a clear day. The grass, once withered and brown, now stood up straight and green. He saw bushes at the peak of their growth, full of life. He saw tall trees raise themselves against the force of gravity to their full height, replete with many sparkling leaves. A rabbit stood up and shook itself as if just awaking from a long sleep, then scampered away happily.

All this Parley saw with his own two eyes and his numbed brain. He did not know what happened then. He vaguely remembered unlocking the cages and leading the animals into the open air. He thought he remembered taking handfuls of seed and spreading them to the wind. All over the world things - living things - were blossoming into a full and fruitful life.

Parley sat down in the dewy grass and thought, while the sun shone down on him at full zenith.

The answer came to him immediately. The Nothing was the end of evolution, the Supreme Intelligence, the Superior Being - God!

Parley's new breed of men, those which would look out for their inferiors, had already been bred, eons ago. And now it jumped from planet to planet, making each world a better place in which to live. For Earth would certainly be a better world without man.

The Nothing had taken the libidos of man, and with them had reinforced the living potential of other forms of life.

Tom Parley was alive. But it did not matter now.

THE ETERNAL ROOM

The wiry old Professor Higgins sat in the laboratory in mute silence, unaware of his surroundings, fitting the last controls on his time travel machine. The machine – a cryotemporal room as it was referred to by the professor – was just that: a room about the size of a small closet, encased in a frame of cooling coils. Liquid helium crawled around the coils, ready for the last bit of energy required to drop the element to a temperature of absolute zero, at which point all atomic motion stops.

Professor Higgins' life-long friend and eminent scientist, Professor Johnson – a tall bearded fellow with enormous hands – strolled into the laboratory and, seeing Professor Higgins hunched over the many control dials, boomed out to him in his deeply masculine voice:

"Professor Higgins, I am going to ask you for the last time. Do you know anything about Lucifer, my prize Siamese cat?"

The wiry professor stated frankly, without a hint of mirth in his voice, "I'm truly glad for that, Professor Johnson. Now that you have asked me for the last time, will you please leave me alone?"

"All right," shouted Professor Johnson indignantly. "All right. Then I am going to sit here and pester you until I receive a civil answer."

If there is anything that Professor Higgins does not like, it is being pestered. So he gave in, but only partially. "Very well. I can only tell you that it is not here, now."

Similarly, if there is anything that Professor Johnson does not like, it is having his cat referred to in the neuter gender. "Lucifer happens to be a female, Professor Higgins. And I am well aware of the fact that she is not here, having searched the house from top to bottom without finding so much as a toenail."

"I don't doubt that."

Professor Johnson thought, then came out with, "Higgins, you are obviously concealing something." All respect had gone out of his voice.

"I am."

"Ah-*ha*."

"But I am not concealing your infernal cat."

"Oh." Professor Johnson thought back, then said, "How can you be so sure that Lucifer is not here?"

"Oh, but she *is* here." Professor Higgins used the proper gender this time, not wishing to get into an argument on that point again.

"But you just said that . . . "

"That she isn't here, now," the wiry professor cut him off.

Professor Johnson fingered his scrawny goatee. He knew that it was a habit of Professor Higgins to be enigmatic. He chose his words carefully and deliberately. "Can you tell me anything at all about the present state of my cat?"

"Yes." That was all. The question did not require an explanatory statement, so Professor Higgins did not offer one.

"What?"

"I can tell you where she is."

Professor Johnson took it coolly. "Where is she?"

"Right over there."

Professor Johnson followed the finger to an obviously vacant spot on the floor. "I don't see her." That was posed almost as a question.

"How observant of you."

Professor Johnson was by now quite peeved. In a gruff tone of voice, he said, "But you just said that . . . "

Again Professor Higgins halted him in mid sentence. "That she is there. However, she is not *now*." For once the wiry professor explained something, even if only halfway.

"You mean that she isn't there now."

"I mean that she is there, but she is not now. Now, if you will excuse me, I am going on a long trip."

"You are not leaving this room, Professor Higgins, until you tell me explicitly all you know about Lucifer's disappearance."

"Quite right, Professor Johnson."

"Qui-quite right about what?"

"Simply that I will not have to leave this room to go on my long trip."

Professor Johnson saw his chance to irk his companion. "You are not planning a very long trip, are you, Professor?" Then several more malicious thoughts occurred to him. "Or are you going to trip and fall on the floor? Or perhaps you will die and begin that long descent to . . . "

"I can do without the witticism, Professor Johnson." It was a habit of Professor Higgins not to allow anyone to complete useless sentences. "Now, if you will pull up a chair I will explain the entire situation."

Professor Johnson glanced about, but except for the cryotemporal room and the stool on which Professor Higgins was sitting, there was not a stick of furniture in the laboratory. Consequently, he remained standing, irascibly.

"Just recently I made a startling discovery in the field of cryogenics," started Professor Higgins, still fiddling with the controls on his cryotemporal room. "Last week I achieved the scientific marvel of bringing a vial of helium to the lowest possible temperature, that of absolute zero. When that happens, of course, you know that the agitated movement of atomic particles comes to a complete halt, and there is absolutely no molecular motion. But, the fantastic part is that the instant the helium touched that point, it disappeared.

"My first conclusion was that the atoms had reverted to a collapsed state, somewhat like the original ylem that existed prior to the formation of the Universe as we know it. However, upon weighing the vial, I found that its weight was decreased by the exact amount of weight of the helium. Therefore, it had left the vial in a very surreptitious manner. That, Professor Johnson, is the crux of the matter.

"After diligent consideration upon the occurrence, I devised my Cryotemporal Theory of Motionless Matter in the Space-Time Continuum. I shall attempt to explain it like this. We live in a space-time continuum. Now, motion is the force behind space – that is, without motion there is no space. And without space – since space and time are reliant upon one another – there is no time, with the net result that by stopping motion, I stopped time. I call this the Anti-Einsteinian Effect.

"For further experimentation I created the cryotemporal room. This is a specially sealed room encased in cooling coils, using helium as fuel. By bringing the helium to absolute zero, it broke out of the space-time continuum by creating a cold field. Everything within this field – if I may euphemize – passed into time. Your cat was in this prototype cryotemporal room."

Lugubriously, Professor Johnson placed his face in his hands. Then, clearing his throat, he began awful conjectures about Lucifer's fate. "Do you mean to say that Lucifer has gone – or is going – through time, and will reappear in the normal space-time continuum in that spot some time in the future?"

"If only that were the case, Professor Johnson," Professor Higgins now felt sympathy for his friend. "Unfortunately, in that early model of my cryotemporal room, once the atoms' motion was stopped, there was no way of causing them to move again. Therefore, your cat will go on through time . . . forever."

"Oh, poor Lucifer." Professor Johnson convulsed with horror, rather than moroseness, or with hatred for Professor Higgins.

"Don't worry, please, dear professor, for by now she must have suffocated from lack of oxygen."

Professor Johnson was beyond reprehension. "I suppose I should thank you for that act of inadvertent humanitarianism," said the bereaved man.

"Look at it this way, Professor. We are scientists,

and as such we should be willing to give up something for the advancement of science."

"Yes. Yes, you are correct. On with science."

Professor Johnson continued with his narrative. "Now, with *this* cryotemporal room, I have built in a heating system so that I can rejuvenate the molecular motion at any time, and re-emerge into the normal space-time continuum.

"Since my machine will be at rest while space and time are going on, I will emerge at this very same spot, but time will have advanced. How effective my room is, or how far I will travel in time in relation to the normal passage of time, I can find out only by personal experimentation. And, of course, I can go only forward in time. There is no reversal of the process, so I shall never be able to return to this time segment again.

"But it is my purpose never to return. For I am growing sick and tired of this world where there is constant bickering and fighting. I am an old man, and I yearn for a Utopia where I can rest my weary bones. I go now to seek a better world. That world must exist sometime in the future. And by diligent and careful search I will find my paradise and live out my remaining days in utter happiness.

"I will leave you now, Professor Johnson. Unfortunately, I can carry only one person in this particular model. However, I am leaving behind the plans and mathematical calculations for the entire project, so if you care to follow my better judgment, please feel free to do so. For now, so long."

On that, Professor Higgins entered the cryotemporal room, and closed the door slowly behind him. He adjusted the valve on the oxygen cylinder, looked over the water bottles and concentrated food containers, and checked the heater which would make possible his return to the normal space-time continuum. Then he began to lower the temperature of the cooling coils.

The wiry professor knew that the process had worked, but he was disappointed in the process. There were no blinding lights, no weird noises, no queer sensations. He had simply slithered out of the normal space-time continuum and into the unreal beyond.

He wondered what would happen if he opened the door now (a meaningless word, he reflected) and stepped out. Probably each of his atoms would be torn out and deposited in a different instant, or segment, of time. His molecular structure would be spread over many years of time. That's me all over, thought the professor, since he was enigmatic even to himself.

After a considerable passage of time, Professor Higgins decided to re-enter the normal space-time continuum and see exactly when he was. He realized that the old house would not stand forever, and if he reappeared at a point in time when another object existed in the locus of his reappearance, the convergence of two masses would create a complete conversion into energy – with a result equivalent to an atomic bomb blast. But he would never let that worry him, for in that instance he would never know what hit him, or what he hit. There were so many dangers involved with time travel, he opined.

He switched on the heater. The helium atoms responded accordingly and molecular motion began. Professor Higgins waited until the temperature was fairly high before he shut down the heater. He grasped the hatch and wrenched it aside. The door burst open and the professor was sucked into the empty void that was outer space.

Professor Higgins was dead in seven seconds.

*   *   *   *   *

As Professor Johnson sat ruminating in the now vacant laboratory (except for the still-warm stool) he began to formulate his own ideas on the Anti-Einsteinian Effect.

The professor said aloud, as was usually idiosyncratic of him, "Poor Professor Higgins. All that talent lost because of an irrational dream. Sure, he was right in assuming that space and time stop – but in relation to the universe as a whole, and not to this room. Ah, yes, he forgot about interstellar motion. The Earth is in constant motion – around its axis, around the sun, around the Galaxy.

"His theory was correct, though. When he emerges into normal space-time, he will have traveled ahead in time, and he will be in the same place. But the Earth will have moved away from that place. He forgot that all things are relative."

Professor Johnson swept away his tears, and lit a match to the plans for the cryotemporal room. Shaking his head, he muttered:

"But we must all give something to science. May he (w)rest in peace."

DESTRUCTION
(or PERSPECTIVE)

It was a glamorous city, thought the people who lived there, its glamour brought into splendid colors by the golden rays of the sun. There was not a cloud in the sky on this particular day. In the center of the city there was a great Pit in which the inhabitants slept, stored food, and took care of the young. The Pit went deep into the earth, spreading out its tunnels so as to make little homes for the individuals. Around the Pit stood an enormous wall made of sand, from the top of which they would be able to defend themselves against attackers, who would kill them and loot their city of its riches.

They worked from the early morning rays of light until the moon and stars shone at night. All day they gathered food and brought it into the Pit; then out again over the wall to search for more. They were happy living the way they were. They had a great deal to be thankful for; they had comparatively safe homes, lovable families, and magnificent sunlight which . . .

Suddenly a great shadow appeared over the city, hung there ominously for several seconds, and then proceeded to plunge downward. It came closer and closer to the city; and as it came nearer, it became darker and larger. With ever-quickening speed it flung itself toward them, completely blotting out the sunlight.

It sent a cold stream of panic and horror down to the innocent little beings which now dropped their food and scurried toward the Pit. Screams echoed from the Wall. Bodies came running in torrents over the Wall. From all parts of the city, a myriad of little bodies ran with only one destination in mind – the Pit. The lucky ones made it deep into the safe interior of the Pit; while others still clambered down the sides; and while still others never made it.

The unknown substance closed down on the city and a few, too few, seconds later, made contact. The city collapsed upon the scurrying bodies. The bodies themselves were twisted and mangled and crushed, The great Wall was completely flattened. Sand and dirt poured in the Pit. Tons upon tons of it compressed itself deep inside of it, thus sealing it off from the outside world.

All was quiet.

John Cider and his son, Dick, had gotten up early that morning in order to go hunting. John held his gun high while Dick skipped happily beside him.

They were walking through an open field in the forest when they came to an ant hill. When Dick spotted this, he immediately put his foot over it menacingly for several seconds, and then struck it down fast.

Dick skipped on through the forest in the glowing sunlight beside his father.

THE COFFIN

Blackness!

Everywhere there was blackness. It lay like a shroud on a bleak December night. In an attempt to see, he strained his eyes until they ached. He blinked hard, but still there was only the nether darkness of absolute and final death.

He gulped, combatting futilely the low humidity of the surrounding atmosphere. He was paralyzed with fear. His appendages were glued to his side, collecting sweat. His heart beat ominously loud in his pounding ears; or was he actually only feeling his heartbeat and unconsciously transferring the sensation to the more physical tympanic membrane?

Were his eyes, in fact, really open? He was sure that they were. Nevertheless, he could not rid himself of the doubt. But surely he was able to discern whether or not he had his eyes open: No, he was not able.

Slowly, torturously, he sent movement into his right hand. (He was sure that his mind was too diffuse to move both hands at once.) Then, he moved his whole arm. He pulled it up over his thigh and along his stomach. So weak was he that the mere pressure of a button on his sports jacket halted its advancement.

He was weak; very weak. Suddenly he felt hunger, and with that suggestion came the feeling of thirst. He swallowed hard and long, but his parched throat was so dry that it hurt. And if he did not stop sweating he would soon die of dehydration.

Again he moved his hand upward, and this time, with deliberate determination, he sent it over his face and let it come to rest on his forehead. He did not bother to wipe off the perspiration, for the expenditure of energy was too great. He stuck his fingers deep into his eye sockets and felt a stabbing pain. He writhed with violent agony. Yes, he had his eyes open. Yet he could not see. Either he was blind, or he was enveloped by a Stygian darkness that was never encountered on the bleakest, moonless night.

The pain brought him back to stark reality. He cringed from it. He was becoming more aware, and he was beginning to think halfway straight. But still his thoughts were foggy and indistinct. Unsorted visions passed before him: visions of fear.

His hand was very tired and it collapsed under its own weight. For several seconds he lay still; then he brought his hand up again. Describing a long arc at arm's length, he raised it. There was a sudden jolt as it crashed into something hard. It fell back limply.

He lay still, fighting off the fear that accompanied that sudden halt. It had scared him so badly that it was all he could do to stop shaking. Desperately he brought up both arms until they felt the rough, uneven surface above him. He ran his hands along laterally until each simultaneously ran into perpendicular barriers.

Then his arms collapsed. By chance, his right hand alighted upon his pocket before dropping to his sides. And in that brief instant of time he had touched something and vaguely remembered what it was. He reached in and felt a slick, metallic object.

Lighter!

He extracted the cigarette lighter and renewed hope surged within him. Fumbling, he managed to flip open the lid and slide his thumb along the revolving striker. But he had to use strength; strength which he was in no position to obtain. He had only his own resources. He struck the wheel hard and a spark appeared – it flickered out as fast as it had come. Again he rubbed the striker – again the spark did not catch.

A rage of anger shot through him; for once since he had regained consciousness his fear had been set aside. He tried again, this time with success. The flame shot up, then shrank to a short pyramid of fire.

As he looked past the flame he saw the ceiling; it was very low, so that it gave him a feeling of claustrophobia. He could plainly see that it was made of wood, for the grain showed up defiantly. For long moments he followed the meandering grain with his eyes, for the simple reason that he had nothing better to do.

Then he began thinking. It was especially hard to think because thoughts usually occurred by reacting to external stimuli; but here there was nothing.

He banged the wooden ceiling – a solid sound returned to his ears. Sound: how long had it been since he had heard a real sound? Days? Weeks? All sense of time was lost to him. The soundless void pounded in his ears, tormenting him. He could not even remember how a sound would sound. He thought that his situation was utterly hopeless.

He rolled over onto one shoulder and, with the lighter in one hand, pounded the wall with the other. The wall was solid. He rolled over onto the other shoulder and, after taking the lighter in the opposite hand, banged again. The wall was solid.

He ran his hand along the grain of the wood, receiving a splinter. He retracted his hand quickly, but did not attempt to remove the small painful particle of wood. The incident was so infinitesimal to him that in the large scale of things it hardly mattered.

The wood was new, freshly cut. Sap still seeped out in many places. He shuffled his feet and met another barrier. He raised his head and bumped it severely on the ceiling. Forgetting the pain, he looked down at his feet. The feeble rays of the lighter just reached the end where he saw another wall. He stretched his neck backward and peered beyond his head – another wall. He felt the rough, wooden floor on which he rested. It was like all the rest. So, he was surrounded by six walls. There was one on every side of him. To him it described some kind of long thin box. He was in a box.

Coffin!

The word rang out in his mind. He screamed in his mind's voice at the very thought of such a perplexing predicament. But no sound came from his throat. He tried to push the idea away; he tried to forget it. But the plain truth of the matter was that he was indeed lying inside a coffin.

That was an unconfirmed statement, he told himself. Perhaps it was just an ordinary box. The absurdity of the situation no longer made him simply wonder. It awed him; it inspired him; it made him shout in terror. (Still his throat emitted no sound; try as he might, he could not utter even a stifled gasp.)

He tried to wipe the sweat off his neck and face, for the salt was stinging him. Besides that, the heat within the coffin – he no longer had the will to deny the obvious conclusion – the heat that was caused by his labored breathing was becoming unbearable. It had always been unbearable, but it did not make itself known until his mind had cleared up. As long as he had been thoughtless and unintelligible, he had not been able to realize what was happening. He had been incomprehensible, and he had let his thoughts pass by.

Time passed. Not much, but to him it seemed like forever.

Then with a mental shout he said to himself, *I am a man.* Suddenly it sounded silly to him. After all, what was man but one of a myriad creatures inhabiting one of a myriad planets revolving around one of a myriad suns burning up its solar fuel in one of a myriad galaxies . . . ?

Ad infinitum.

Myriad!

He tried to forget that meaningless word. He tried to think, to remember, to be more specific about his origin. Gradually, thought pictures began to materialize from a mist of obscurity. A wild, silent phantasmagoria unrolled itself before him. . . .

He saw himself driving down a long country road that was studded with leaf-filled trees. The beautiful rays of the sun were reflected and refracted through atmospheric moisture. The grass was alive with scintillating dew. A cool breeze swept over the roofless red convertible and into his face, passively lifting his hair and laying it down across the top of his head. The sky was blue. White puffy clouds were scattered across the firmament, as if they had been plucked from cotton fields and placed there. It gave him a feeling of immensity, the large sky resembling the interior of a painted dome.

Yet amid all this intense beauty, something was wrong. The needle on the fuel gauge had fallen below the empty point, and the car's engine was kept alive by the spare gasoline that was not registered by the instrument.

Ahead was a farmhouse. He knew that farmers who lived way out in the country usually kept their own supply of gasoline, since it was such a long distance to the nearest filling station.

He turned into the driveway and jumped out of the car. He strolled nonchalantly toward the house. He knocked on the door and turned away so that when it was opened he could act surprised. But there was no answer. In his dream he saw his mouth open, his lips move, as if he were shouting, but no sound came out. His dream was so quiet, so tranquil, so serene. And so tormenting.

Obviously there was no one home. He steadied his eyes across the rolling fields and into the deep, dense forest. He saw no sign of human life, no motion at all. So much the better.

At the end of the driveway, near the barn, he saw a large red tank. Furtively he glanced around again. Then he took the pump handle and let his car drink its fill. When the tank was replete, he rewound the hose and replaced the pump handle.

Suddenly he jumped around and stared at the young girl. There must have been a sound that warned him of her coming, but in his dream he could not hear it. She was about eighteen, dressed sloppily in blue jeans and loose-fitting shirt. Her long, black hair trailed down her back. She might have been pretty if she had been washed and dressed properly.

Everything moved quickly, and his numbed mind was barely able to keep up with events. He grasped only the essentials of what followed.

The girl drew a wisp of hair away from her eyes and spoke. He answered. She spoke. He advanced on her, obviously sweet-talking her. She was reluctant and afraid, and took a step back. He leaped and grabbed her shoulders. She struggled and tried to free herself. He uttered soothing words. She still resisted. He shook her, but not too violently. She eased up. He placed a hand on one of her breasts, and thrust his other hand between her legs. Then she screamed a silent scream and broke his hold. He tried to hang on, but he had only a weak grip on her shirt. It tore down the side and fell partly away, exposing a bare shoulder that her tresses failed to cover. He instantly regretted his rash act.

A farmer stood suddenly in front of him. The girl ran to the man and cried, cringing under a strong protective arm. The man's face bent into an odd contortion of hatred. The farmer must have been the girl's father; at least, the graying hair and facial lines would lead one to believe that the age difference made the relationship highly probable.

What was worse, the farmer was pointing a rifle at him. It looked like a .22 caliber, although he was not familiar enough with guns to be certain. He was in a tight spot, and the farmer's gaze made it look tighter. He was afraid. He had not really meant to harm the girl. He only wanted to talk to her, to look at her, to . . .

He had just gotten carried away. As those thoughts came to mind, he saw the man in the dream – the man who was representing himself – gesticulating and chattering, but to no avail.

The enraged farmer pushed the girl aside and pointed at the ragged edge of her shirt, meanwhile moving chapped lips. Again his own lips moved futilely as he tried to explain the accident and the sorrowful circumstances. The farmer raised the gun, and in abject fear the stranger turned and ran for the woods.

The farmer will not shoot an unarmed man in the back, he told himself over and over. That would be cold-blooded murder. Surely the farmer could forgive him for some loose emotions and minor indiscretions.

Faster and faster the dream moved along, until it was almost a soft blur before his unwilling eyes. Silently he saw himself running; he had almost reached the woods. Somehow he sensed that the farmer was raising the gun. It seemed that he was an imaginary spectator watching the tragic end of a play. He knew what the farmer was about to do, a fact which made the situation more unbearable. He knew that even now the bullet was hurtling out of the gun barrel, even though he heard no telltale report. He saw a frightened man so close to the trees which would afford safety from impending disaster.

The scene changed, and he saw through the eyes of the pursued stranger. The forest was just in front of him; fear was behind. He knew, like one who has already seen a play, that he would never make it to safety. He felt a sharp pain in the back of his head; it pushed itself deep into his skull, spreading blackness in its wake. He felt a numbness creep over him. Just before ultimate oblivion swept him away from reality, he saw the ground rush up to his face – it never reached him.

Nothing!

He was awake. In his excitement he had dropped the lighter and was momentarily plunged into darkness. Involuntarily, his hand had moved to the back of his head in search of the wound. His index finger rubbed over the spot where before a prominent occipital protuberance had projected, and found only a deep, circular hole.

In horror he withdrew his hand and cringed in dread anticipation. He tried to curl up into a ball, but the cramped confines would not allow it. He opened his mouth to scream, but no sound came out – this silence was going to send him mad. He had to hear something – anything. He opened his mouth wide, and pounded on the floor until he wilted from exhaustion. Then he lay still.

He gasped, sucking in dry air through his gaping mouth. The horrible thought of death ran through his mind. According to his dream he should be dead. A bullet had penetrated his skull. The terrifying thought came to him.

Was he in fact dead? Could this be death?

He felt his heart throb. He felt his lungs reach out in an attempt to get more air. He felt the sting of sweat on every square inch of his bony. These were his sensations; this is what he felt. He was very much alive. Yet he had been buried.

Had the farmer unknowingly buried a man he thought to be dead, so that there would be no evidence? Or had that old cuss knowledgeably interred him alive, banishing him to suffer his final minutes in an agony so horrible as to defy description?

There was room in his mind only for hatred. He aimed most of it at the accursed farmer who had had no reason to be so excitable; the execrable farmer who had shot him; the detestable farmer who had built a coffin and placed him inside and buried him knowing all along that he was alive and breathing!

Air!

He thought of it quite by accident. Now he realized his dilemma. Soon he would use up all the oxygen in the small coffin, and he would be left with only carbon dioxide and nitrogen, and he would suffocate and die of oxygen starvation. He imagined the excruciating anguish of not being able to fulfill his want for air. It would be an empty feeling. He would gasp, but there would be no oxygen. He would twist and turn in agony. He would lose hold of his mind. His bloodless fingers and toes would go numb. Then his arms and legs would lose all sensation. His mouth would open wider and wider, groping for something that was not to be had. His body would go into convulsions. He would shake and shiver. A black envelope would cover his head – the same blackness that had killed him once would come back to haunt him. He would have to go through that awful cycle again. He would have to die again . . . and again . . . and again. . . .

The fear of death was imminent in him, and his necrophobia would most certainly cause his death.

The sooner, the better, he thought. *Hurry up and die, worthless body – die. Die. DIE!*

Suddenly his necrophobia brought him back to reality. Actually, he had a strong will to survive: not so much because he wanted to live, but more because he was morbidly afraid of the alternative.

Calm yourself, he thought. *You must stay calm.*

For the first time since he had regained consciousness, he had thought a rational thought. It was miraculous. Reason had returned to him. Now he had to keep control of it; he had to stay alive.

For what purpose? he thought. *To wreak vengeance on the world, and on the farmer.* That in itself was enough willpower to keep him alive.

He scrounged around on the floor until the familiar lighter was safely in his hands. He struck it and forced the flame to stay alive. Then he rolled over and surveyed the situation. He pounded on a loose board and immediately saw a way to make good his escape. He hit it and hit it and hit it. At least he was making noise. Sound was such a comfort to him; he had almost forgotten how to hear.

The board moved, and optimism reigned in his hopeless mind. He pushed and pulled, twisted and turned, until the board broke off and there was a hole in the side of the coffin. He stuck his fingers into the soft dirt and gripped the next board. He pried it with a madman's strength and tore it loose from the securely nailed frame. That gave him a hole about a foot long and eight inches high. Not enough. He pried another board loose in practically no time. That took down the whole side of the coffin for the length of nearly a foot – just enough room for him to squeeze through.

The feeble flame of the lighter was gobbling up oxygen, but he feared that he would die if the flame flickered out. He put the lighter in the corner of the coffin by his head, where he could not knock it over inadvertently as he dug, or douse it with soil.

He grabbed handfuls of dirt and pulled it close to his chest. It was very soft, having recently been dug up. When he had quite a pile of dirt gathered around his chest, he compressed it into a lump and shoved it into the depths of the coffin. There his feet took over the job and smashed it down, out of his way.

Loose dirt fell through the ragged opening in the side of the coffin. With his massive hands he began to dig a great hole. He did not know it, but there was a fair amount of loose air trapped in the dirt. And he could use every available molecule.

When the hole was large enough, he stuck his head out of the coffin and pulled out his torso. He clawed the dirt and it fell on him. The situation was revolting. Dirt found its way inside his shirt, up his sleeves, and down his pants. It filled every facial orifice, but he did not bother to brush it off, except for his eyes. He shoved it into the coffin with abandon born of desperation.

He ignored some of the minor hindrances. He ignored the salty sweat which made the dirt cling like glue. He ignored the splinters which dwelt deep in his hands. He ignored the broken finger that he had smashed against a rock. He ignored the total discomfort of the heat, and the diminishing air supply, and the fear and hatred which he held pent up within him.

For all his efforts he had made a sizeable hole. First he crawled into it and sat up. He dug. Then he pulled himself to his knees. He stuck his fingers into the dirt and let it fall on him and all around him. He had to ignore all these things, for his life depended upon it.

His dirty hair fell across his face and into his eyes. He brushed it back and continued working. How deep would he have been buried? Regulation depth was six feet. He probably lay no deeper than that, for the farmer would have had no reason to believe that he could dig himself out of the ground. He reasoned that if he were perched on his knees, he had about two feet left to reach freedom. That meant two feet of loose gravel which only had to be undermined and it would fall down. An easy two feet.

Now he could almost stand in the hole. He worked harder and faster, rocks and stones becoming more and more prevalent. He placed his hands solidly on the ground and pushed it upward. He felt it give away, but could not hold it. The dirt mounted up and fell back. In his anxiety, he lost most of his senses and began shaking. He told himself that a little patience would soon get him out of here.

He dug away some more dirt, then pushed again. This time the dirt went high into the air. Suddenly his hands fell away into a huge open space. He set his feet and forced his muscles to give him strength. His head erupted from the hole; he sucked in great lungfuls of air. Next his arms slithered out. He placed his hands strategically and with the last ounce of power propelled his body out of the ground. He kicked and climbed and scrabbled until he was able to sit on the edge of the hole. He yanked his legs out and rolled over and over until he was many feet away from the makeshift grave.

Redness!

A fiery, glowing redness emanated from the very air. As far as he could see there were only wispy clouds of redness. Flames licked up from the ground, emitting terrific heat. It was as if a veil of undulating fire had been placed over his eyes.

As he gazed out into the empty, infinite vastness, he perceived a lone shape that was approaching him. Its own redness served as protective mimicry against the same colored background, making it barely perceptible. But it moved!

Indistinctly he saw it coming closer. The shape was still vague, but a hint of recollection advanced with it. He tried to think, to remember why he had that feeling of familiarity – of déjà vu. As the shape grew more discernable, so did a creepy feeling of horror.

The red mist cleared and the shape became discernible. It stood like a man; it was a man's height; it had a head and arms and legs affixed proportionately on its body. But there the similarity ceased. An extra appendage arose from the base of the spinal column, terminating in a spearhead. Its face was adorned with a pair of short, stout horns which sprouted from a receding forehead. Plainly it was the Devil.

Satan, Lucifer, Beelzebub – and the hundreds of other aliases that it used – came toward him. The beast was grinning in pleasure, and its eyes gloated, growing larger with each successive gloat. Something was behind those dreadful eyes. They seemed to shout at him, telling him a long story.

Then it dawned on him. Yes, he had died, from a bullet wound in the back of the head. And after death he had been given the choice of supreme content, or descending to the land of torture. Unwittingly, by digging upward, he had chosen the latter.

And for his sins, he must cleanse himself. He must again and again dig his way through the earth until that awful indecency that he had performed on that innocent girl had been erased from his memory and he himself felt that he had been purged of evil.

The Devil pointed a finger at him and banished him to the endless repetition of death.

Blackness!

Everywhere there was blackness: it lay like a shroud on a bleak December night. In an attempt to see, he strained his eyes until they ached. He blinked hard, but still there was only the nether darkness of absolute and final death . . . and eternity.

THE BALD REVOLUTION

I didn't realize how tired I was until I woke up on the bus, when I knew instinctively that I was near my stop. I squinted my eyes, but it didn't help much. I knew that I shouldn't have taken Lois, my wife, to the movies last night, but she had insisted and, after all, it was the last night for the show. So today, Monday, I suffered the consequences. I could hardly wait to get to the office where I could catch up on my sleep.

The boss was out on a two-week vacation. Coupled with *my* two-week vacation coming up in August, that meant that I got a full month vacation every year.

I pulled the buzzer cord and found my way off the bus without disrupting too many passengers – especially the standing sleepers. They're the worst kind. I looked at my watch and saw that I was five minutes late already, and so instinctively I began to run. About halfway to the office I remembered that the boss was on vacation, so I immediately slowed down to a lazy stroll. I soon found my way to the building. I went through the lobby straight to the coffee shop.

I saw some of the girls from the office their having coffee. I decided to stop and say hello. I picked up a cup of coffee from the counter – I hate this cafeteria-style coffee shop – and sat down with them.

Sue, the tall brunette, was talking wildly, as usual, to Barbara. However, when I sat down and greeted then in my usual fashion, she immediately turned and said to me, "Sam, have I got news for you. Do you know that the latest hair style for women is to have no hair at all?"

I had read about it in the newspapers, and had talked about it with several neighbors over the weekend, but I knew that telling her that wouldn't stop her, so I did not even try.

"They take a razor and shave your head clean."

"Yes, it sounds very sanitary," I said.

"Can you imagine going around with no hair at all on your head?" That was directed more to Barbara than to me.

Barbara shook her hear in a disgusted manner. "It's just awful."

"I suppose the new advertising gimmick will be, 'Hate that gray? Shave it away,' " I quipped light-heartedly.

"Very funny," said talkative.

Before I got myself any deeper into trouble, I excused myself and made my way to my office. There, for the next three hours, I slaved away at the work that should have been done last Wednesday. Tomorrow I was planning on doing Thursday's work, and on Wednesday I was going to be very busy doing Friday's work. That left me Thursday and Friday to clean up this week's work, because the boss was coming back next week.

At lunchtime I went down to the coffee shop and ordered a roast beef sandwich. I looked around for the girls, but could not find them anywhere. That in itself was very strange. But stranger still was the fact that nowhere in the entire coffee shop could I find a feminine figure. I saw Davis, my replacement in case I should be ill and not be able to come to work some day.

"Davis," I called. He brought his lunch over to my table and sat down. "Davis, where are all the girls? I haven't seen any since I got here. And you know that Sue and Barbara are always at the same table talking."

"Oh, weren't you here when it happened?" He acted very surprised, as if it was common news.

"When what happened?" I stammered.

"It was at the ten o'clock coffee break," he began. "I was down for my usual Bromo-Seltzer and soda water – you now, I have a chronic migraine and I am continually taking that because it's the only thing that seems to help."

I failed to understand how Bromo-Seltzer could reduce the pain of a migraine, but didn't bother asking. Davis was, well, different.

"The girls were gabbing as usual, when suddenly every one of them ups and complains of a headache and that she cannot possibly continue to work that day. So every one of them walks out of the coffee shop and right out of the building. Then for twenty minutes it was murder to get back to the office because the elevators and stairs were jammed with girls complaining of headaches. I even heard they were using the fire escapes to get out of the building. Man, it was really weird."

I was stunned. The probability of every office girl – from secretary to scrubwoman – getting a headache at the same time was so infinitesimal that it was practically impossible. The first thought that came to my mind, before I fell completely head over heels for the story, was that it was a hoax – that Davis was trying to pull my leg.

"Say, you aren't kidding me, are you, Davis?"

"I wish I were. It gives me the creeps to think that this thing ever happened."

I had finished my roast beef sandwich so I excused myself and went back to my office. I soon brushed the idea out of my mind – without explanation – and tried to get down to work. Five o'clock came early, which in itself is odd, and although I had completed another day's work, I was still three days behind.

On my way downstairs – our elevators move much too fast for me to enjoy – I heard more than one man mention the strange phenomenon. Still the halls were devoid of girls. It wasn't until then that I realized how much I had gotten used to having girls around. I guess I had taken them too much for granted. Well, I would make up for it by buying flowers for Lois.

There was a flower shop just down the street, on my way to the bus stop. Again I was thunderstruck by the fact that there was not one female on the streets. I went into the flower shop and looked around for the cashier.

There was no one in sight. Then I remembered that the proprietor was a female. That seemed to have some bearing on the fact that the store was empty. I picked out an arrangement that was colorful, and left the money on the counter.

I saw the bus coming so I ran down the street to meet it. I saw that there was a fairly large group of men waiting to get on, so I allotted myself time to buy the evening edition. I threw a dime on the outside counter and picked up my usual paper, not bothering to read the headlines. I just made it to the bus stop before the doors closed and I leaped on board.

After making my way to the back of the bus and not finding a place to sit, I was resolved to stand. About fifteen minutes later I squeezed off the bus and for the ten thousandth time vowed to get a car – a small car, to be sure, perhaps a Volkswagen, but at least something to get me out of these maddening bus rides.

Once on the street I saw my other bus exchange coming down the street, so I had no time to open my paper. But I did have time to notice that not a woman was in sight, nor were there any on the bus that I had just gotten off of. I raced to the stop and boarded the second deathtrap. It was just as crowded as the first, so again I resolved myself to stand. Well, I thought, at least I will have plenty to read tonight.

Exactly thirty-seven stops later I got off and headed in the direction of my apartment, where I knew Lois would be waiting impatiently for me. Sadly I noticed that the streets were bare of women, even the old hags who stood out on their doorsteps and stared surreptitiously at every stranger who happened by. The only thing that kept me from going insane, I think, was the fact that I had the prospect of seeing Lois soon.

I reached my apartment building and began climbing the long stairs to the third floor – this elevator, too, was too fast for my tastes. Hurriedly, almost running, I found my apartment and rushed through the door.

"Honey, I'm home." I shouted.

"I'm in the kitchen, Dear," she answered.

I threw the paper on the table and eagerly walk into the kitchen. On a day like this even my wife would be a welcome sight. I veered around the corner and was halfway into the kitchen when I fell back in surprise. My mouth dropped to the floor. My shoulders sagged what little they were able. I seemed to lose my balance and I found myself falling backward until something got in my way and I fell heavily into a chair.

"You – you – you're bald," was all I was able to say.

And it was true. My wife – *my* wife – stepped out of the kitchen, her bald pate shining and reflecting the light.

"Of course, Dear. It's the latest style."

I looked at her, speechless. There was nothing I could do to rectify what had already been done. Somehow I could not bring myself to believe that this was really happening – that it *had* happened! I was so dumfounded that I could not even think straight. But the thought persisted that it was all false, that it was a dream, or that she was trying to scare me by wearing a wig. Yet I realized the truth. She had had every follicle shaved off her head.

"But – but we were talking about it just yesterday and you said that you wouldn't be caught dead like that."

"But Dear, that was before the Call."

"The call? What call?" I stammered.

"What is the matter with you? Did you give up reading the paper on the way home?"

She acted surprised, as if everyone in the whole world knew about the Call except me.

She took the paper off the table where I had dropped it, and tossed it on my lap, face up. I stared at the bold headlines, which read: WORLD WOMEN START BALD REVOLUTION.

I explained to her that I hadn't had time to read the paper tonight because of the crowds on the bus.

"Well, I'll explain. Do you remember Doctor Mabel Reynolds, the genius who some years ago invented a telepathic projector? Well, she had her own private fortune and she decided to expand her projector to a greater scale. All these years she's been working on it, trying to complete it before she died, because she is the only one who can understand the principles.

"She finally finished it. That was two weeks ago, and ever since she has been testing it on small groups, until she was absolutely sure that it would function properly. Then came the news of the new sales gimmick – the shaved off head. Naturally every self-respecting female was revolted at the very idea of such a denudation.

"But it gave Dr. Reynolds the perfect solution to her problem. You see, with her machine she can drop post hypnotic hints which simply must be obeyed. She had planned on using her projector in some fashion which would solve the world crises – like projecting to everyone that war is awful and should not exist; then there would be no war. Or she could project that everyone would act neighborly to their fellow friends and not do anything that would not be suitable to someone else's tastes; that way she could rid the world of crime completely. Then came the default. She found that her machine was not powerful enough to implant deeply into the minds of men. But on women it worked perfectly."

"You mean that she can make people do anything she wants them to do, just by projecting to them?" I was appalled. "In the wrong hands that could be disastrously dangerous, couldn't it?"

"Right, but she is the only one who understands the principle behind the projector. So it was absolutely safe to fool around with, because Dr. Reynolds is completely altruistic in her thinking. Now, to continue, she could only control the minds of women, which made her objective very difficult to obtain. Then she saw the Way. The widely publicized report of the new hairless style gave her the perfect idea for how to achieve her goal. She projected to every women in the world (including Eskimos and Aborigines and Bushmen and Polynesian islanders) that they should get a baldie -

that is, have all their hair shaved off. Of course, like she planned, no one could resist. But she is not that heartless. Along with that order she projected the reason, so that it made every woman *want* to get a shave, besides just making us get it. The Call came at nine-thirty five this morning."

"That must explain the reason every girl in the office building complained of a headache and left – to get a haircut."

"Yes, that is the only drawback – and a mild one it is – of the projector: it produces a mild headache. Yet, it served its purpose in providing an excuse to get those girls out of work and down to the barbers."

Gradually I was becoming more accustomed to the fact that my wife's hair was gone and there was nothing I could do about it. My wife's soothing voice helped to ease the pressure somewhat. "And what is the plan?" I asked.

"Ah, yes, the plan. I was just coming to that. Well, first, tell me how I look to you. I mean, am I beautiful, or ugly, or repulsive . . . "

I turned my head away as the feeling of an oncoming vomit entered my throat.

"Yes, definitely repulsive. But that is as it should be. Now you will see the light. Dr. Reynolds did not go to all this trouble because she has stock in a wig factory. No, it is much simpler than that, especially to you, since you are a man. Here is the proposition, or rather, the ultimatum. The female sex has long played the part of the underdog in the world. The sole purpose of the Revelation – or Revolution, if you wish to call it that – is to breed equality in the world.

"Let me go deeper than that. If you don't do what we tell you to do, we're going to keep our heads shaved. Now the things we want you to do are: stop all kinds of fighting, including wars, revolutions, and just plain meanness; and the female of the species gets absolute equality. By these two means we hope to abolish all kinds of inhumanities. From now on the human race will act as one individual, instead of a number of warring countries. Do you agree?"

I looked at her for a moment, then turned my head disgustedly.

"Or would you rather be married to a bald woman for the rest of your life?" she added, a twinkle in her eye.

There was nothing for me to do. I could not refuse, because I knew that every female in the world was bald, and I could not stand to see a hairless woman. Weakly, I nodded my head, saying, "But for goodness sake, go out and buy a wig until your hair grows back."

She smiled. Then came the awful moment – or rather, eternity – when the orders came hard and fast. "First of all, we'll have to rectify the house cleaning situation. Now we'll work this on a weekly basis: I clean one week and you clean the next. In the eating situation, I'll cook, because you get home too late to cook, and you will wash and dry the dishes. Any other difficulties I came across, we'll fix when they come. But I want it understood that we – meaning the females of the world – are not taking advantage of you men. We just want everything to be even-steven. Okay?"

I was still too weak to speak, so I just nodded my self-contained approval, unwillingly.

Now the terrible crisis is over. The women have control of the world, although they call it equality. They never threaten to go home to mother when the spouses have an argument; they simply threaten to shave off their hair. And, by golly, the system works.

Of course, some good came out of the whole experience. There are no more wars, because the women have been conditioned, or hypnotized, against it, and the men are afraid of what the women will do. But they run the country pretty well. Crime is abolished – almost. Everyone is very friendly, like one would expect to find in a quaint country village. In short, the world is a living paradise. Only we men have to work harder for it – for you see, what women call absolute equality is nothing more than matriarchy.

They say that everything is equal. For instance,

they cook, we wash and dry dishes; they clean house one week, we the next; we make money, they spend it.

Yet never once have any housewives offered to go to work and earn some of the money for us to live on equally, while we stayed home and watched television.

CRABS

My name is Robert More and I am a reporter. When the story began, I was on vacation at the sunny Atlantic City beach in New Jersey. I did not want to see another typewriter for the next two weeks. But as it always happens to a reporter, I was on vacation when the big scoop came.

Tall, billowing waves were crashing on the multitude of defenseless swimmers. I was sitting on a sand-filled beach towel with an inflatable surf mat in my hands – without air. So what could I do but start huffing and puffing? I have powerful lungs and a lot of air – most of it hot – so that in five minutes I had the thing almost bursting, and myself as well.

The sand burned my feet as I strolled across the beach to the water. It was icy cold. I had not planned on being completely inundated, but then I had never counted on stepping on a crab and tripping face first into an oncoming wave. That was one of those unpredictables that I've heard so much about lately.

Well, anyway, I finally battled my way beyond the wave barrier and I thought I would sit tight until a really big one came along. Sometimes you can see them forming way out in the ocean; but most of the time those kind break apart by the time they get near the shore.

I was lying lazily on the surf mat with my feet up in the air when I heard a hissing sound directly behind me. As I turned my head, I thought about the many times that I had checked the mattress for air leaks, and that it could not possibly be that. It was.

There was a long greenish thing lying across the mat. At first I mistook it for a weed. But it was as stiff as a board – and anyway, what kind of seaweed can punch a hole in an air mattress?

It was not a weed. The thing was about a foot long – that is, the part that was above the water. As my hot air leaked out, I debated on whether to try to pry it off or not. If I did, more air might leak out; but I didn't have much time to think, for another greenish thing came out of the water from the other side and attached itself to the mattress. The situation was definitely getting out of hand, and I was plenty scared. Then the worst part happened, and I'll swear on a stack of Darwins that it's true.

A pair of eyes emerged from the water and stared me in the face. Not human eyes either. They stood on long, slimy stalks, without brows, lashes, or lids. Behind them soon followed a large carapace, some five to six feet across. Around this carapace eight sturdy legs grew out. I realized then that an enormous blue crab held my gaze.

A crab of that size could just as easily slice off my head as it could sneeze. (Do crabs sneeze?) If I say I was scared, I'd be lying – I was petrified. I could only stare at it in disbelief.

Fortunately, the sinking surf mat brought me back to reality. I splashed into the water and, gasping and choking, clawed my way to shore. I must have made more noise than a barrel of monkeys and probably swallowed more water than said barrel could hold. I did a combination of swimming and running when I hit shallow water. I dragged myself up on shore and ran to my towel. I did not mind so much the gritting sand, now.

Had I been dreaming? Was it a figment of my imagination? I'm a reporter, remember? I am trained to observe things accurately and notice details. But the details are what scared me. Maybe a six-foot crab sounds a little weird. Of course, I've heard that somewhere off the coast of China or Japan, or maybe it was Alaska, spider crabs get to be as much as four feet across, at the shell. But this was ridiculous.

I debated with myself about whether I should tell someone what I had seen, letting people know that I was crazy, or keeping mum, and letting them only *think* I was crazy.

There was not much debating. I chose the lesser of two evils and kept mum . . . for about five seconds. Then a gasp escaped me as I, as well as a hundred other people, saw it emerge from the waves.

It was a machine about the size of an automobile (and not these fancy sports models, either.) It was a flat contraption, seemingly without a roof – then I saw that it had a glasslike, transparent dome, which readily reflected the strong glare from the sun. Seated upon this vehicle, within the dome, were two giant crabs. One was up front, operating levers and handles, while the other sat in the back doing nothing. The rectangular car moved on tanklike treads. It measured about twelve feet long and six feet wide; the top of the platform rose scarcely more than four feet from the ground.

Around me, screams and shrieks arose from the lungs of many terrified people. But the crabs did not seem the least bit perturbed. They sat majestically atop their tank and wheeled it up on the beach. Pandemonium reigned. Half mad with fear, men, women, and children took it upon themselves to vacate the immediate and surrounding area. I got more sand kicked into my face than I could get in an hour of a full-scale desert windstorm.

When the dust settled down, I was the only one on the beach except for the three tanks. I blinked, and rubbed my eyes. That didn't change it. Where one tank had stood before, three were now lined up neatly. They advanced slowly, still spurting water from several holes in their sides. The six giant crabs eye-stalked me over. I was scared. What could I do but run? Nothing that I could think of at the moment. So I ran, kicking up sand as I went along – only there was no one there for me to carry out my revenge on.

I reached the car and fumbled for the keys inside the pocket of my swimming trunks, opining thankfully that I kept them there. My fingers shook like a waist reducing machine, but I managed to get the keys out of my wet pocket and into the hole for which it was intended. Once inside the car, I sat thinking. Momentarily I had forgotten how to start it. When I remembered, I did it so fast that I stunned myself. I started to leave when I noticed a young couple having trouble with their car.

I shouted out the window, "Jump in."

How long had it been since I had last spoken? I don't know, but my voice did not sound the same as it used to. I unlocked the door and they scrambled in. I took off so fast that the acceleration made me feel like I was on one of those crazy roller coasters.

Now where could I go, I asked myself? Try the police station, I answered myself. That was the perfect solution. And with these two witnesses to back up my story, they had to believe me.

Why are policemen always so obstinate and hard to convince? I've been a reporter for a long time, and I've never been able to figure that out. I decided that since there might not be many policemen at the station, I'd better pick some up. Going seventy miles per hour in a thirty-mile-per-hour zone ought to get at least a few. It did. And going through a red light picked up another. A motorcycle cop took off after me when I went through a stop sign. For numerous other violations, which I care not to mention, I had quite a train after me. By the time I reached the station, there were four police cars and three motorcycles lagging behind.

I started pumping the brakes about a block away, and even then I almost passed the station. I stopped the car in the middle of the street, opened the door, and climbed out in one graceful motion. Then I remembered the pair in the back seat. I turned around and threw open the rear door and let them flow out. There was a horrible stench oozing from the car. Brother, what a time to get an upset stomach! Well, I'd have to tend to that later.

I helped the two limp forms into the police station. The commotion came just after me. A bunch of cops waving ticket books poured into the room. There was so much noise that I could hardly hear myself think.

"QUIET!"

The police chief had an exceedingly loud voice. Calmly he said, "Now what's going on here?"

More shouts. Not a word could be deciphered.

"QUIET!"

That was in the same monotone as before, but with more feeling behind it. "Let the gentleman explain, since he seems to be the cause of all this trouble."

He meant me. I had to make it sound good. I said, louder than in my usual voice (when had I last heard myself speak like myself?) "Giant crabs came out of the ocean riding tanks. They came up the beach and headed for the boardwalk." Not too convincing, was it?

"What?" said the chief in disbelief.

Well, what could I expect him to say. After all, it was the common answer.

Then, in a change of attitude, "What's this guy accused of?"

He obviously did not hear a word I said; either that or he pretended that he didn't.

"Speeding."

"Passing through a red light."

"Going through a stop sign."

Et cetera, et cetera, et cetera . . .

"Quiet!"

Needless to say, that was the chief. "You went through an awful lot to give me this story, didn't you, Mister?"

"But it's true," I said defensively. "I swear, every word of it is true. Look, I've even got two witnesses to back up my story." I looked for them, and found them. But they did not look like they were going to do much backing up. The girl had passed out; she was still on her feet because the crowd of cops were pressing against her so hard. And her husband . . . ?

Hardly anyone noticed the telephone, but some attentive cop answered it and through the din shouted: "It's for you, sir, from Snider. Says it's important. Sounds scared."

The chief battled his way to the phone, with the hounds on top of him telling what bad things I had done. He looked at them hard, and before he had a chance to shout his by now famous word, you could have heard a pin drop.

"Yeah. . . . Yeah. . . . Yeah. . . . What? . . . Are you crazy or drunk? . . . Are you sure? . . . Okay. . . . Okay. . . . But wait – . . . Snider? . . . Snider? . . . " He slammed down the phone and shouted, half to himself, "He hung up on me." He scratched his head and, turning to us, said: "This guys story checks out. Snider says there are giant crabs riding tanks up the boardwalk. And I had to join the police force?" A pause. "Well, don't just stand there. Let's get a move on."

There was a mad rush for the door and I was caught just about in the middle. Shouts of frenzy and disbelief rang out.

"Giant crabs? Really?" That sentence alone was uttered by each cop at least half a dozen times.

"I sure do love to eat crabs."

"You'd better watch your step, or they're liable to get even with you."

We poured into the street. A great crowd of people were already there, trying to make a report. They shouted about being invaded by flying saucers; about monsters from outer space; about fantastic ray guns. Some even got as close as to say that there was an overflow at Cindy's Crab Inn. The chief ignored them all.

I was ushered into the street. A startled cop who was on his way in was whirled around several times before he saw me.

"Hey! I gotta give that guy a ticket for running a stop sign."

"That and a million other things. Where've you been, buddy?"

Everyone piled into cars. Cops set their sirens on. The crowd was terrible. You'd almost think that the whole boardwalk was there. I only know that the whole boardwalk was not at the boardwalk.

I climbed into my car along with some motorcyclists. Three of them crammed into the back seat.

"Hey! What's this warm, smelly stuff I'm sitting on?"

"Shut up and move over."

I pulled out between two police cars and together we took off for where the crabs had last been seen. We had to fight our way there, but we made it eventually. The closer we got to the boardwalk, the thinner were the crowds. The boardwalk was emptier than it was at four o'clock in the morning. Not a person could be seen in either direction. We got no closer than a block to the place. The crabs' location was not known now, since there was no one stupid enough to be on the boardwalk watching them.

"All right," bawled the chief. "I want every gun out and ready to shoot."

"Hey, you're not going to kill them, are you?" Maybe I sounded a bit silly, but it suddenly came to my mind that they had not hurt – or attempted to hurt – one single person, and so far they had not done any damage. That is, except for puncturing my rubber raft. And I forgive them for that. No, I am not touched in the head.

"Naw, were gonna play footsie with them." He said that slowly and sarcastically. The cops were diffusing themselves over the area. We did not know exactly where the crabs were at that time, and no one had enough nerve to go look for them.

No one except me. And I kept mum.

I've been called a crackpot before – never a hero, just an impatient madman. After the first few times it doesn't hurt as much. Of course, I was not about to go up to the crabs and say, "Take me to your leader." Or, "I come in peace" That stuff is for the birds.

"What are you going to do now, sir?" I added the "sir" so I could get on the chief's good side. There was little or no respect behind the utterance.

"We're going to sit tight until I get orders."

"Then you won't mind if I mosey down a bit and see how things are going?"

He ignored me and said, "You know, you got a pile of tickets behind you."

I ignored him and said, "You know, I'm a reporter, and I can't wait to write the story of how the Atlantic City Chief of Police single-handedly kept the crabs at bay until reinforcements arrived."

He laughed and said, "Sure." Then he acted nonchalant and began issuing orders in his well-known froglike voice. I simply wandered away.

I came to an alley, and when I was sure that no one was looking, I ducked in and ran along the pavement. The alley led directly to an old house and then branched out perpendicularly. The house stood on stilts. You know, so they won't get their little toesies wet in case of flood. I slithered under the house and scrambled across the sand. The house met the boardwalk with no way to get out. So, I went under the boardwalk and came out on the far side, not a hundred feet from the ocean.

Cautiously I raised my head and peered, first right, then left along the boardwalk. There, about half a block away, stood the three tanks, parked in front of an old dilapidated building. And all along the boardwalk were little circles of water, leading right to the peculiar suction cups that made up the tank treads.

The crabs were nowhere in sight.

I never walked such a long half block in my life. But then, I never walked half- crouched for a half block before, either. In the sand, just opposite the tanks, I stared at the building. A dusty, dirty sign hung overhead: THE MARQUIS JOINT.

I'd never been there, but it did not sound like much. (I thought, What possible reason could the crabs have for visiting such a place?) I climbed out of the sand and onto the boardwalk, still crouched. I felt tingles all over my body, and my heart made an audible throb twice a second. I ran to one of the tanks and hid behind it. I was almost too afraid to go on. But a scoop is a scoop, even if I *was* on vacation.

The door was wide open, but I could detect no movement inside. I ran on tiptoe to the doorway and sneaked one eye around the corner. Except for hastily abandoned pool tables, the room was empty. My knees began to shake, but I had to go on. If I stopped here my editor would kill me.

I stepped inside the room. A board creaked, and I swallowed hard as my heart left my throat. Nothing happened. I stood absolutely still. I could hear a faint noise from the back room. It sounded like beeps and squawks, probably from the crabs. And then there were little cracks every once in a while, like the constant crackling of knuckles. Do crabs have knuckles?

There were two doors, but the telltale trail of water lead to only one of them. So that's what crab tracks look like, I thought. I had never seen them before.

Silently I crept across the room to the door. It was slightly ajar. This made me even more cautious. With a sudden burst of speed I ran to the door and flattened against the wall. Am I out of my mind? I thought. I don't know what made me do it, but I hope I'm never that irrational again.

I peered through the crack and got a good perspective of the entire room. The six crabs were huddled around a long thin table. One sat at the head while the others lined the sides. It took only that one glance, then I ran like the wind out of the building. I went right down the boardwalk and eventually into the chief.

They tell me I was stark raving mad. Of course, I don't know, but upon reflection, I am inclined to agree with them. They shipped me off to the hospital and after a couple of days in a straight jacket and a padded cell (they were taking no chances with me) they let me go and I wrote my story for the paper.

That's just about the whole story, except for the end, which I have never told yet. But now that I am married and prestige does not matter that much anymore, I can let the crab out of the bag. Everyone knows that the crabs got away, and were never heard of again. Nobody knows how or when they left, but when it was later investigated, not one trace of their having been there was found. Many psychologists leaned on mass hysteria.

But I know different. I know the truth.

You must understand why I could not tell anyone at the time. They had me locked up for three days afterward as it was, and if I had told them what I had seen in that room, I would still be in an asylum. Besides, considering my distressed mental state, I doubt that I would have been able to articulate the story in my usual smooth professional manner.

I had discovered the secret of the crabs. I knew their terrible mission.

But how could I have told the world that the giant crabs had come here from someplace deep in the sea to – roll dice?

THE GAME

Andrew Harper meandered along the busy city street, not quite completely inebriated, but intoxicated enough to trip over his own feet. He was a sight for all humanity. His face had two-day-old beard stubble on it, his hair hung down in front of his face, his tie was loose, and his shirt was hanging out of his pants. All in all, he looked like a typical drunk.

But there was the irony, for he wasn't as drunk as he would like to have been. He had already visited three bars this morning, yet still he was plagued with the awful memory reminiscent of the previous night. And he wanted to forget that. For last night he had learned, or rather formulated, the Ultimate Truth.

The achievement of Truth was the goal which mankind had always sought. Now that goal had been achieved by one man, Andrew Harper – much to his chagrin. For the Ultimate Truth was so wild, so terrifying, so improbable, yet so real, that he had not been able to comprehend it and stay sane. So he had decided to get good and drunk in an attempt to forget. But so far it hadn't worked. He still remembered.

He shuddered as the thought assailed him again.

Through half-conscious eyes he glared at the bright neon sign that protruded over the sidewalk several feet away. It was a taproom, and lazily he made his way toward it. He knew that he was going to have another rough time, for drinking had never come easy to him, so he had been resigned to stay away from it. Nevertheless, he seemed to have a natural immunity to intoxicating beverages – at least that was so this morning. Or perhaps the Truth was so strong that no amount of drinking would make him forget.

The terrifying thought entered his mind, and with renewed will he set off at what to him was a run, for he had not much strength left in his beaten body. Sincerely he hoped that this time the drinks would have the effect of pushing him out of reality. Better to suffer the agony of a thousand hangovers then to remember the Truth.

In front of the bar some quack was preaching to a non-existent audience about the sin and evil of drinking – alcoholic beverages, that is. The man himself looked like a sot. His hair was unkempt, and his clothes bedraggled. His teeth were a dull yellow in appearance, as if he hadn't brushed them for a very long time. Possibly he was a bum. More likely he was a drunken bum. All in all, Harper might have been looking at himself a few days from now.

"And I tell you the truth," the old man shouted, "when I say that there is no greater sin than imbibing the drinks of the Devil, for you can never wipe out the memory that you are the Lord's creation to do with as He pleases. Only the Almighty controls your body, for your body is His, since He created all life. And although your body is His, your soul may go to Hell."

As he spoke, he constantly slapped his right fist into the palm of his left hand. The old man's arms swung wildly, and several people were forced to make a wide detour around him for fear of being clubbed.

Harper, interested in the conversation that the preacher was having with himself, and resentful of it, walked up to him and in a cracked voice muttered, "You're a filthy old man. And a liar to boot."

With that his legs gave out from under him and he collapsed onto the sidewalk. The old man bent over to help him up, but Harper didn't feel like being handled. "Listen, Preacher, I don't need any help from you. I can get up by myself." His voice was amazingly calm for a man in his condition. Wearily he made his way to his feet and grabbed onto a lamppost for support.

"I don't know what you think you're doing," Harper coughed, "but you are absolutely wrong. Drinking is good for the soul because it makes you forget. And right now all I want to do is forget. And your silly preaching isn't going to stop meeeee – " His voice whined out as he slipped down the lamppost and sat down in the street again.

The preacher, utterly stunned, dropped his mouth wide open, revealing two rows of yellow-stained teeth.

Harper continued to sit in the gutter. He stared off into nowhere and talked aimlessly. "I want to forget because last night I learned something that makes all your preaching a complete waste of time. And I want to forget that terrible secret."

The preacher found his tongue after a few thoughtful moments and resumed his cool, preacherlike attitude. "Young man," he said, although Harper was not a very young man; it was just that the preacher was a very old man. "You must come to realize that drinking is not the solution to your problem, whatever it is. You must face the facts and understand them as best as you can. Drinking will only make it worse when you again find out that you cannot run away from something."

So he was an honest-to-goodness preacher after all, and not just a run-of-the-mill street bum.

"Preacher, if you knew what I know, you wouldn't waste your time preaching. You would go into a room and put a gun to your head and pull the trigger. That is the only answer to my problem, but I'm too weak to do it."

"To solve all problems you must first pray for forgiveness, and then perhaps you will find the right path again."

Harper looked glassy-eyed at him, and pulled himself out of the gutter. "So, you think you can solve my problem, don't you? Well, let me tell you something, I'm not the one with the problem, because I know the Truth. You are the stupid one, suffering in your little fantasy world, playing with your idols, preaching your 'words for the wise.' Now I'll give you a word for the wise that you can think about: life isn't worth living."

With that Harper proceeded to walk into the tavern and make his way to a nearby stool. He sat down at the counter and waited for the bartender to arrive. He ordered. He drank. He ordered. He drank. He ordered. He drank. Again he ordered, but this time he did not have time to drink, for the preacher sat down next to him and pushed the glass away.

Harper looked up and said, "Well, did you have a talk with your spirit? Did he tell you to come in here and 'save' me? I'm beyond saving, so go peddle your wares somewhere else."

"A disciple of the Lord is never at a loss, for I have Heavenly help."

"Yeah, sure you do. But if I need a new soul I'll go to a shoe repair shop." Harper meant that sarcastically and not as a pun.

The old man disregarded it, and said, "If you will talk over your problems with me I might be able to help."

"Look, Buddy, ever since I found out the Truth last night I've been trying to forget, because its too vast for the human mind to comprehend. All I want to do is forget . . . forget . . . forget . . . " His voice trailed off in a sudden fit of weakness as his head lolled and hit the countertop.

The preacher bent low to Harper's ear, and said, "I can help you only if you will open your mind to the truth and let the Lord enter."

Harper picked up his head, pure hatred burning in his eyes. "All right, if you're in such a quandary to know, I'll tell you. But let me warn you, you'll be very sorry at the end of the discussion that you ever asked me."

Assuming his role, the old man said, "As a disciple of the Lord I am especially suited to listen to the sad tales of bleeding hearts."

"I just hope for your sake that you know a good psychiatrist and can get to him fast," said Harper. Then he took a deep breath and began his tale of quiet horror.

"I often pondered about the immensity of the Universe, and it has always bothered me that there is no end to it – that it is, in fact, infinite. As far as the largest telescope can see, space just seems to go on and on, never ending. But then, how could it end? Would there be a wall, or an invisible barrier? No, because there would still have to be something on the other side of that wall or barrier. And suddenly I was overcome with a feeling of smallness. I could imagine, to a certain extent, that man inhabited only one of millions of planets, which revolved around an infinity of suns, which in turn congregated in an infinity of galaxies, which then could then be grouped into universes. I broke down and cried because I could not imagine such a thing as immense as all that; and because I could not find the limiting factor, because there is no limit to space, or time; that they went on forever.

"Then it came to me. How could man, who is such an unimportant part of this vast scale, be of any significance? All of a sudden I knew that man was nothing; not just a small part, but absolutely nothing. And if man were nothing when compared to the Universe at large, what possible purpose could life have? But already I knew the answer to that. There is no purpose. That is the Ultimate Truth. There is no point of living because we serve no purpose – there is no goal.

"And what's worse, I know I'm right. I've studied, and I know. Life is simply a haphazard arrangement of atoms and molecules, which were thrown together by accident in the primeval ooze and which then thrived to maintain a meaningless existence, all to no end."

Harper had done it; without breaking down he had spoken the Ultimate Truth. It was difficult, to be sure, but he had done it. Again his head lolled and careened toward the countertop.

"But all men live for the purpose of serving the Almighty – "

"Don't hand me that superstitious stuff," shouted Harper, sweat rolling down his forehead. "It's all phony. Man invented it because he couldn't cope with reality, and a pointless existence. So in desperation he made up a purpose, and passed the buck to an imaginary being. Well, the game is over, and your lies and deceits are falling apart under the stress of scientific knowledge. And we are right back to where we started from a million years ago – back to a pointless existence."

The preacher looked downhearted and stared woefully at the glass that he had taken away from Harper. He shoved it back in front of him. "It must be hard to live with something like that. Even if it is a false conception, it must be awfully hard to feel completely lonely and unwanted. I pity you."

"No!" screamed Harper. "I pity *you* for being so blind and stupid, and for not realizing the Truth when it is shoved right under your deceitful nose. You are to be pitied for your ignorance." Harper gulped down the rest of his drink.

"And you are to be pitied for your knowledge."

Harper disregarded the last statement, for he knew that this preacher was so close-minded that it would be a waste of time to try to spread the Truth through him. He slipped away from the counter, throwing down some bills to cover the cost of the drinks. And even such a simple act as that seemed infinitely minimal and pointless to him. He made his way to the door, the preacher close behind him.

"Perhaps if you would consent to be indoctrinated into the House of the Lord," began the preacher, "I could make you believe that life is not as you think. Perhaps I can make you realize the real fulfillment and the gaiety of living."

"Save your lies and your brainwashing and your idolatry for some dope who is too ignorant of the world to be curious about the Truth. There is nothing you can do to help me except kill me."

He went through the door and into the full sunlight of high noon. He looked at the people scurrying in the streets, and he knew that they meant nothing. He looked at the buildings towering above him, representing the greatest achievements of mankind, and he knew that they meant nothing. And finally he looked at himself, and against his deepest wishes he knew that he meant nothing.

As he hung onto the lamppost for support, the preacher shook his head, for he felt very sad that he had not been able to help this poor man out of his misery. And perhaps he realized that the Truth had too long been obscured, and that there was, in fact, no purpose to life. This is what becomes of the unbeliever, thought the preacher.

Harper looked up at the sun, hitting him full in the eyes, and shook his fist defiantly, shouting to the world, "There is no purpose to life."

Suddenly the sun went crazy, as if in exaltation. It grew fantastically large: double, triple its former size, until it filled the entire sky. Then it reached out for him, and humanity, and all life, and in a final surge of unequalled power it crushed the Earth beneath its terrible grip.

Oblivion.

G— and S—— were huddled over the intricate machinery with which they had just created an atom. It was difficult to bring the convecting currents of energy together to form matter, but it could be done in this world of advanced technology. Then came the even harder part of producing just the right conditions to create life. Yet that too could be done with apparent ease. For G— and S—— were playing the Game.

On their atom they first created a source of light. Then, by atomic manipulation, they caused the oceans to become separated from the land. Then came the awful waiting that always accompanied the Game. For hours they cooled the atom which they had created out of nothing – that is, if pure energy could be called nothing. Then, when it was sufficiently cooled, they mixed subatomic particles until they hit upon the right formula. The amazing transfer had been made. They had created life!

Slowly the simple life forms evolved. First came bacteria. Then simple but self-sufficient plants spread throughout the world, soon followed by parasitic animals. They divided and re-divided mutagenically into many and various forms, but to date all were single celled. After a while, when life had reached a fairly advanced stage of development, the single cells began to aggregate into colonies, which in turn became one microorganism consisting of many parts. Many millions of years later, according to the time scale of the atom, life took on more intricate forms. Now multicellular organisms ruled the atom, covering the entire wet portion of it. But that was not enough.

Life spread to the dry parts: first the plants, and then, like before, followed by parasitic animals. And once there, they did not stop evolving. Insects evolved into higher types, which, although they were not as well suited and less adaptable, nevertheless spread over the continents. Yet still life had to take its slow course of evolution.

Fish became amphibians, and amphibians became reptiles. For many millions of years these fearsome reptiles ruled the land, and to some extent, the water. They spread into almost every kind of imaginable niche, attained innumerable sizes and shapes. And their main objective was specialization, which, although good at first, soon proved to be their downfall.

The steady course of evolution continued, leaving the giant dinosaurs to death and extinction. Mammals took over the scene. These too took on many varieties, but they maintained their adaptability to a certain extent. Then evolved the perfect specimen, for it was in the image of its creator, G—.

Yet that did not solve the problem, for there were far too many animals inhabiting the atom, and this might cause the downfall of the perfect animal, Man. So G— and S—— froze the atom four times in quick succession, killing off most of the unwanted and undesirable elements. Ice ages left Man the supreme ruler of the atom.

At this point in the Game, the tension began. G—, who was playing the part of Goodness in this particular Game, fought to keep man alive and faithful. He impressed upon their minds the evil portrait of S——, so that they would fear him and not confer with his evil ways and thus reverse the polarity of the Game. For in *this* game, S——'s purpose was to disease the minds of Man so that they would resent the graven image of G—, whose form they took in the course of their evolution. All he had to do was to make one individual completely faithless in the face of G—, so that the man resented his image. Then he would have won the Game.

But the allotted span of time given to S—— to do this feat was almost over, and it seemed that G— would win. Then, to save the day, the treasured moment came. Just a few years before the Game would be lost to G—, one infinitesimal organism detached itself from the crowd and defied the Supreme Will, which had heretofore been enforced. He had absolved himself completely from the Faith which G— had invested in him, and by the narrowest of margins, S—— won the Game.

At that moment they shut off the generators which had kept the atom alive and had prohibited it from lapsing into a state of pure energy, which it had originally been, and it fell into oblivion. Yes, the Game was over, and they had destroyed their artificial world!

The Game had taken five grueling hours to play (five thousand million years according to the time scale of the atom), and both the contestants were tired. G— said, "You play the Game well. Perhaps some day you will make the championship."

"Thank you," replied S——. "But I admit that it was very close, and for a while there I thought the Game was lost."

G— smiled and said desperately, "I will beat you the next time, though. Just because you have taken three in a row does not mean that you will continue your streak of luck. However, the next time, let me play the destroyer, and you be Goodness. Then I will test your versatility and adeptness and we shall see who prevails."

"Ha-ha-ha-ha," laughed S——. "You will find me just as challenging in that roll as well." S—— stretched out his cramped and tired muscles. Five hours bent over a machine, using psychic powers to the fullest extent, could not be called relaxing, although he played the Game for enjoyment.

"You now," started S——. "Ever since I began playing the Game, I have been wondering if perhaps they are not so very wrong after all."

"What do you mean?" asked G——.

"Have you ever thought that there might not be a Creator? I mean, after all, I never did much buy that story about the Creator who, out of pity for the lonely Universe, made our world so he could give something unique to posterity."

"That is blasphemy," shouted G——. "Of course there is a Creator."

"I am not so sure any more. I have been studying very hard lately, and I do not think that there is such thing as a Creator. Our learned astronomers would have us believe that there is life on other planets, yet we are supposed to be unique in the Universe. I think that the Creator is a sham made up by fools and founded on superstition. And this Game has made me only more confident that I am right. And now that I have said it aloud, it seems even clearer to me. There is no purpose to life."

"Be quiet, before you evoke the wrath of the Creator. You do not know what you are saying. The Game has affected your mind, and you are having delusions as an aftereffect."

"No, you are wrong. I am fully conscious of what I am saying, and I mean it. There is no Creator and there is no purpose to life."

"Do not say that," pleaded G——.

During the conversation they had walked outside. S—— looked up at the sun, hitting him full in the eyes, and shook his fist defiantly, shouting to the world, "There is no purpose to life."

Suddenly the sun went crazy, as if in exaltation. It grew fantastically large: double, triple its former size, until it filled the entire sky. Then it reached out for him, and humanity, and all life, and in a final surge of unequalled power it crushed the Earth beneath its terrible grip.

Oblivion.

Afterword: If God created man, who created God?

THE RED SANDS OF MARS

Prelude

Once, with spirit in their hearts, men sought to con-
    quer space,
And with this end in mind they started out to find
    their place
Among the stars, across in time, the Universe to see;
New suns to chart, new worlds to climb – a new phi-
    losophy.

1

The ship came plunging from the stars
And crashed upon the sands of Mars.
And when all of the dust had cleared,
The lone man fumbling with his beard,
Because his helmet had been split
And he could only think and sit
While all his air escaped from him
Between the cracks so small and thin.
He died without heroic cheer –
For Mars contains no atmosphere.

2

A second Martian ship was sent
Because man's will was still intent
Instead of fighting useless wars,
In conquering the red sands of Mars.
The survey ship was not to land,
But rather send a robot hand –
A programmed probe with modifications
To carry out the explorations.
The expedition was not in vain –
For man would return to Mars again.

3

Another ship met with a splash
When into storms it whipped and lashed.
And as the inundation fell
The crew filled up the ship's dry well.
The men rejoiced, but then they wept,
Because they suffered with regret
That overwhelmed by such a thirst
They first went mad and then they cursed
The fate that rated such a rank
By poisoning their water tank.

4

An expedition of three men
Had crashed abruptly on Mars when
A freak of Martian atmosphere
Had distorted their radar gear.
The ship was torn from stem to stern
But man's strong will had kept the burn
Of Mars' desert heat behind
The will of a subconscious mind.
Through hardships fierce the men lived on,
New civilizations yet to spawn.

5

A rescue ship, not far behind,
Brought hardest men of the same kind,
Along with quantities of food,
Machines and tools and guns and crude
Provisions for a basic camp
From which man hoped that he could stamp
Upon the Martian sands in peace
Carrying weapons for surcease
Of war that had blighted the Earth
Thus showing Nature man's true worth.

6

The greatest parasite of all
Had come to Mars in spite of all
The hardships that had to be endured
In living on the ancient sandy shore.
The sand was hot; the sand was cold;
The bell of death frequently tolled
When a precious life was lost
Due to dryness, crystal frost.
The world man picked was hard indeed,
But bearing hardship was man's creed.

7

So man lived on in plated domes;
A giant world with little domes
Who had no choice. They had to live
On Mars' sand and try to grieve
Over a planet that had succumbed
To a manmade terror – the atomic bomb.
A home did not exist for those
Who strained to stand up on their toes
And in the sky see the brilliant brand
Reflect its light upon the sand.

8

A faithless heart; a faithless soul –
A creature living in a hole –
A being set on self destruction –
A scourge, a blight, a malediction –
A thing called man, but better still
A monster that had yet to kill
Its own creator. Man had met
The Universe without regret.
He left, returning to the womb, and
There was nothing left but the sand.

THE POSSIBILITIES OF LIFE ON VENUS

Thesis: Life on Venus is not only possible, but probable.

I   Certain Conditions are necessary for the beginning of life, and different forms are taken under these conditions.
    A   The beginning of life is dependent upon the conditions.
        1   Conditions depend on three variables.
           a   Life cannot really be defined.
           b   A precise range of surface conditions are needed.
           c   Certain elements are specified.
           d   The temperature range is fairly wide.
        2   The continuance and evolution of life depend on changing conditions.
           a   Surface conditions are liable to change.
           b   The temperature may fluctuate.
    B   Living organisms possess the ability to adapt.
II The conditions on Venus are very different from those on Terra.
    A   The atmosphere has some of the same elements as in our own, but they are in different proportions.
        1   Carbon dioxide is very abundant on Venus.
        2   The presence of water has been detected from studies in a balloon.

       3 There are several other gases which contain oxygen.

       4 Oxygen is very scarce on Venus (i.e., free oxygen).

  B There are many ways to determine temperature.

       1 The dense atmosphere reflects, holds, and distributes heat.

       2 *Mariner II* did not account for some important variables on Venus.

       3 New methods of determining temperature have been developed by radiotelescopy.

  C Under the above data, certain theories have been formulated.

       1 The Greenhouse Model makes Venus look very hot.

       2 The Aeolosphere Model makes Venus look very dry.

       3 The Ionosphere Model works on the assumption of a large magnetic field.

       4 The Oceanic Theory supposes that Venus is covered by vast oceans.

III Life can exist under Venusian conditions.

  A The conditions necessary for life are about right on Venus.

  B Life can assume many forms, and can adapt to almost anything.

  C Life may have evolved all the way to insects.

  D Life on Venus would have adapted to its specific conditions.

  E Intelligent life is not likely on Venus.

There is an important difference between life and nonlife; although the differentiation between living things and nonliving things, between organic matter and inorganic matter, is not as clear-cut as biologists would like it to be. There is no definition of life. The different behavior of matter in life may be called "vitalistic." But this means nothing: it is only a name and not an explanation. (1) Usually, life is taken to mean certain molecules which have the ability to absorb other molecules, and thus can grow, and replicate molecules exactly like the original. However, crystals have this same property, and yet they are never spoken of as being alive! Therefore, there is no accurate description which makes life distinctive from nonlife. It must be taken for granted.

Life, in its beginning stages, might seem very tenuous and stringent. True, there are certain and precise conditions necessary for life to begin, and grow, and evolve. It is not something that always was, and surely not something that always will be. To grasp this concept, it must first be understood how life on our planet began.

About two billion years ago, some three billion years after the formation of our planet, surface conditions were very much unlike those that exist today. Owing to the conditions of its formation, the surface was very hot. Water that was squeezed out of the ground was immediately vaporized into the atmosphere. After a long while, the atmosphere became overcondensed with water, and so it began to fall – to rain. After many thousands, and possibly millions of years, this process eventually cooled the land and formed vast oceans. (2) And so a largely water covered surface was the result.

Water also played an important part in the formation of the early Terran atmosphere. Along with water, the air was made up mostly of ammonia (NH_3) and methane (CH_4). Any water reaching the upper layers of the atmosphere would be decomposed by ultraviolet radiation from the sun into its component parts, oxygen and hydrogen. The hydrogen, because of its extreme lightness, would escape the gravitational field of the planet and fly off into space, leaving behind the oxygen, which reacts with ammonia and methane thus:

$$2O_2 + CH_4 \text{ yields } CO_2 + 2H_2O$$
$$3O_2 + 4NH_3 \text{ yields } 2N_2 + 6H_2O$$

Because water is a product, this reaction is self-sustaining. But once vast quantities of carbon dioxide and nitrogen were formed, water would be driven down to join the oceans. But under intense ultraviolet radiation (there was an ozone layer to protect the planet at that time) the products of these reactions, carbon dioxide and nitrogen dissolving in water, would mold themselves into simple hydrocarbons: acetic acid and glycine. These latter two are materials from which the porphyrin ring is constructed by a living organism, and could have been combined in the dead ocean, significant because some of the most important enzymes contain porphyrin as their workers, a definite stepping-stone toward life, although not self-sustaining life itself. Also chlorophyll, the key compound in photosynthesis, is a porphyrin. This series of events was proven in an experiment by Melvin Calvin. (3)

Thus it is seen that the most important elements responsible for the beginning of life are carbon, hydrogen, oxygen, and nitrogen (with trace amounts of sulfur, potash, phosphorus, soda lime, etc.). (4) (It has been suggested that life can exist on different cycles, such as the silicon cycle. Silicon would be favorable at high temperatures at which carbon compounds would break down. (5) However, Dr. Asimov has proved that there are so many other unlikely conditions necessary for silicon existence, that, at higher temperatures, life forms based on fluorocarbons with liquid sulfur taking the place of water, or at lower temperatures, life forms based on nitrogen chemistry with liquid ammonia taking the place of water, appear to be more likely. (6) However, it is the carbon based forms with which I am concerned here, since that represents our own chemical makeup.

For this kind of life, the suitable temperature bounds are limited by the need for liquid water, somewhere between 0°C and 100°C. But at high temperatures molecules are disorganized. In Yellowstone National Park bacteria have adapted themselves to live in the hot springs at 75°C. This must represent the upper limit, while the lower limit is bounded by the freezing point of water. (7)

This is a brief outline of the conditions necessary for life. Of course, in the beginning, free oxygen was not as vital as it is to us today. In fact, it has been proven by Miller, in an outgrowth of Calvin's experiment, that original life forms provided energy for life by fermenting anaerobically (i.e., in the absence of oxygen). (8)

After about a billion years and life was pretty well on its way, conditions began to change. Because of voluminous plant life and their photosynthetic methods, oxygen became more and more prevalent in the atmosphere, and set up the path for animal life. But in doing so, the anaerobic viruses could no longer exist, although they might exist symbiotically or parasitically. The way back was sealed, and life must continue from here.

In time the original simple hydrocarbons were built up into complex organisms called cells; and cells formed colonies of cells, each better adapted to its environment better than the simpler substances. Evolution was in progress. Under new conditions, such as lowering temperature, presence of oxygen, made life move on faster. There was also something new, called predatory rule. Organisms that could not live under these new conditions, or could not adapt to them, died; while those with advantageous adaptations survived and became the progenitors of the succeeding generations. This "survival of the fittest" is important in the evolution of life. Since the weaker organisms died, only the stronger and more capable ones lived. This eventually populated the Earth with many varied and specifically adapted organisms, each with its own mode of existence. They adapted themselves to every possible condition, until all the niches were filled. (9)

Such was the situation on Terra several billion years ago. Now let's move the scene up to the present, and the place to Venus. Venus has always been called the "twin sister" of Terra, because of its external differences, e.g., likeness in diameter, density, and relative closeness. But this is a far cry from the truth. In fact, Venus really has very little similarity to our own world.

The atmosphere of Venus is very dense; at least, the part we can see. Actually, the dense cloud layer begins at a height of forty-five miles above the surface, and extends upward for seventeen miles. (10) The composition of this atmosphere is one of great controversy, and involves an extended discussion.

Previously, the only thing known about the atmosphere was its superabundance of carbon dioxide, which was thought to be the sole constituent. (11) That there is carbon dioxide in the atmosphere is pretty certain, although improved methods have found the existence of other elements, too. The trouble is that the dense cloud layer prohibits observation of the lower, and true, atmosphere. With new instruments, like the spectroscope, this has been pretty well cleared up. Now, scientists even question the age old idea that the clouds are carbon dioxide. It has been proposed that the atmosphere may contain mainly polymerized formaldehyde (CH_2O) in long chains. This is plausible on photochemical grounds (12) by the following reaction:

$$CO_2 + H_2O(g)$$
in the presence of ultraviolet light yields
$$CH_2O + O_2$$

Even though *Mariner II* is reported to have found great quantities of formaldehyde, (13) the spectrum of the oxygen released in the reaction has not been found. Besides, oxygen would absorb the ultraviolet light needed to make the reaction go. Also, the idea of formaldehyde chains involves the existence of droplets of ordinary plastic, meaning that Venus may be enshrouded by plastic. However, logic and incomplete evidence lean away from this point of view. (14)

There is mounting evidence of the presence of water in Venus' atmosphere. The clouds were first supposed to be made of dust particles, but they appear to be too white. And partial clearing indicates the presence of rain, whereas the high velocity wind needed to keep the dust particles in the air would not leave time for it to settle, and thus account for this clearing. (15) Furthermore, any water below the tropopause is relatively safe from dissociation by ultraviolet light because it cannot get through the intense cloud covering (16), and because it is absorbed by carbon dioxide in the Schumann Region (the region at which the temperature begins to decrease with increasing height) (17) One reason water cannot be detected is because there is too much of it in our own atmosphere to blind our instruments. (18) The final denouement came when a manned balloon, armed with a 16-inch Schmidt camera and a spectroscope, rose to a height of 80,000 feet, above the interfering water. By testing the infrared spectra, emission bands matched up exactly with those of ice crystals, and definitely proved that the amount of water in Venus' atmosphere is about four times as much as in our own. (19)

Reviewing back to the section devoted to the primitive atmosphere of Terra, a startling similarity is seen. Some scientists believe that Venus is in a stage of atmospheric evolution similar to that of Terra in the Carboniferous Era. The condensed clouds in the Venusian atmosphere may represent such an uncondensed ocean, still vaporized because of Venus' higher temperature. (20)

So far, oxygen has been neglected in this discussion. As to date, no evidence has been found which purports that oxygen exists in the free state (a fact which is also coherent with the theory that Venus has primeval atmosphere). Spectroscopically, dinitrogen tetroxide (N_2O_4) (21) and nitrogen (22) have been discovered. Also, photodissociation of carbon dioxide near the occultation level may lead to the formation of a carbon suboxide polymer haze (primarily C_3O_2). (23) This could explain the absence of oxygen: it is all bound up in compound. Yet there is a strong belief that oxygen may exist in the free state below the dense cloud covering. Here I quote Firsoff's magnetic theory:

> "Cases differ in magnetic susceptibilities. Some are paramagnetic and are attracted by a magnet; others are diamagnetic and are repelled by it. It so happens that Oxygen is the most strongly paramagnetic and carbon dioxide the most strongly diamagnetic of all gases. The forces involved are small, but if combined with the thermal effect they should lead to a definite tendency for the carbon dioxide to rise above the oxygen." (24)

This means that although we observe only carbon dioxide, the lower strata may be surprisingly rich in oxygen. Thus far, the only real evidence of oxygen in the atmosphere is "ashen light," a phenomenon on Venus similar to our auroras. In spectrograms of these, emission lines have been found which support the existence of oxygen in the free state. This also proves the existence of nitrogen and carbon dioxide, since ionization may take place only in the presence of these elements. Accordingly, a substantially terrestrial quantity may be presumed. (25)

Another point of controversy about Venus is the measurement of its temperature. The most obvious thing noticeable about Venus is its closeness to the sun (.7233 A.U., or sixty-seven million miles) (26); because of this it receives twice as much heat as we do. However, in this respect, the dense atmosphere serves a trifold purpose. Firstly, most of the sunlight is reflected and thus serves as a shield from the deadly solar radiation. (27) By the same token, any heat that managed to get through would be bottled up and unable to leave.

(28) This is the so-called "greenhouse effect." But also in this respect, because the atmosphere is turbulent and has strong convection currents (29), it should distribute the contained heat evenly around the planet. (30)

It is generally presumed that Venus is hot. Spectroscopical and optical observations usually obtain a high temperature, much more than the boiling point of water. This was lately confirmed by *Mariner II*, which comes up with a surface temperature of 426°C, the cloud layer having a base temperature of 95°C and a top temperature of -60°C (31) This implies that with increasing depth there is increasing temperature.

This is confirmed by radiotelescopy. In 1956, the U.S. Navy paraboloid was used during Venus' closest approach, at wavelengths of various centimeter range. At 3.1 cm and 9.4 cm a value of 800°C was obtained. Later observations at .86 cm wavelengths gave an uncertain value varying between -2°C and 300°C. This indicates that shorter waves originate at cooler regions than the longer waves. (32)

At this point three important variables may be introduced. One is that nonthermal radiation may account for some of this heat. For instance, water clouds can emit electromagnetic radiations that have nothing at all to do with heat (e.g., lightning). "Such radiations could make Venus look twice as hot as it really is," says Plummer, of Strong's team. (33) The greenhouse effect may also help to account for some of it. Heat can be absorbed at all wavelengths, but emitted only at higher wavelengths, thus leading to the belief that the accepted values are not a true measurement of heat, just the concentration of high wavelengths. (34) Lastly, the outer temperature can be pretty accurately determined since there is nothing intervening to throw off instruments. This is somewhere around -60°C. Now, because cold air has a tendency to fall (while hot air rises), and the slow rotation would drastically reduce centrifugal force, descending air currents would cool off the surface and regulate the temperature of the planet, much lower than observational data would say. Thus, it might not be any hotter on Venus than an exceptionally hot summer day in Washington, D. C. (35)

In view of the previously stated data, certain theories, or models, of what Venus might look like have been built up. In the Greenhouse Model, solar radiation absorbed by the atmosphere is trapped inside, thus raising the possible surface temperature to 375°C (36). The outer atmosphere will have a lower temperature of -53° to -38°C), so that ice crystals can exist high in the atmosphere. Accordingly, the surface is dry, calm, overcast, and hot as an oven, reddened by the dust which constitutes the cloud layer. (37) The Aeolosphere Model (region of the wilds) suggests that the atmosphere below the visible clouds is extremely dry and arid, kept in motion by chronic, hot, dry winds from above. In this model the atmosphere is made up of calcium and magnesium carbonate dust, fine as talcum powder, raging over a surface where there is no sunlight; only heat, wind, and dust. (38)

The Ionosphere Model proposes that the temperature, measured at centimeter wavelengths by radiotelescopy, refers to the ionosphere. This means that Venus has a highly ionized outer atmosphere containing a large concentration of free electrons, obtained from the sun because of the planet's relative closeness, and held in place by an intense magnetic field which is reportedly five times that of Terra. (39) This will be opaque to radio waves and transparent to shorter waves, thus making the temperature recorded at long centimeter wavelengths come to an overly high value. Experimental proof indicates a moderate surface temperature of 28°C and an ionospheric temperature of 375°C. (40)

Although the previous hypotheses extend from our knowledge of the atmosphere, there yet another which relies on our knowledge of the surface, leading to the composition of the atmosphere. The Oceanic Theory presumes a surface covered entirely with water, and populated with scattered islands, rather than extensive land masses. (41) This explains many of the observed conditions on Venus. For example, because there is very little land exposed to the air, it prevents carbon dioxide from reacting with silicate rocks (42), like in the following reaction:

$$MgSiO_3 + CO_2 = MgCO_3 + SiO_2$$

Thus it explains the abundance of carbon dioxide in the atmosphere. (43) Another excellent proof of this theory is Venus' exceptionally slow period of rotation. Although it has not been accurately determined, it cannot be less than thirty days. This is pointed out by the Doppler Effect (Red Shift), which would make the point of the planet moving away from us shift to the red, and the point moving toward us shift to the violet side of the spectrum. Since this effect has not been detected, it follows that the rotation is too little to be perceived by our instruments. If Venus were covered with oceans, the tidal effect produced by the sun, causing the water to abrade the bottom of the ocean, would act as a retarding agent because of friction of the tides. (45)

All this evidence points toward Venus having an atmosphere similar to that of Terra at about Cambrian times, some five hundred million years ago. (46) At that time there was very little oxygen in the air, vast amounts of carbon dioxide (47), and primitive oceans replete with living organisms. (48)

It might be said that "conditions are right" for life on Venus, either beginning or evolving. All the necessary ingredients are present. The elemental prerequisite, COHN, the four basic elements, are in abundance, as is the necessary compound, water. The temperature, although still uncertain, is very likely within range. Even with all the minor differences, life on Venus, having once gotten its start, would have produced modifications to accord with the planet's surface and atmospheric aberrations, whatever they might be. (49) For instance, where on Terra plants evolved which used sunlight to take oxygen out of the carbon dioxide molecule, and thus produce sugar later in the process, on Venus they would have modifications for extracting oxygen from dinitrogen tetroxide (N_2O_4) or formaldehyde (CH_2O) or carbon suboxides, etc.   In fact, the intense ultraviolet light from the sun, more intense before the carbon dioxide layer was built up to protect the planet (as ozone protects us), because of Venus' closeness to the sun, would cause a faster rate of mutation, leading to a widespread diversification among the local denizens.

As an example, let me cite some Terran examples of diversification. The bacillus Boracicola and some sulfur bacteria can exist easily and comfortably in a saturated solution of boric acid. (50) Some other bacteria, in the quiescent state, have survived after being subjected to a temperature of -190°C and then immersed in boiling water for hours. (51) Some bacteria can break down and rebuild substances; some decompose dead materials; some absorb nitrogen in the air and convert it into useful materials (e.g., nitrates in the soil, upon which other organisms can grow). And what's more, all this can be done in the complete absence of sunlight. Some forms are nourished by rocks which they literally eat and break down into soil. (52)

Thus it is seen that oxygen and sunlight are not prerequisites for life, as is commonly believed. Indeed, two forms of sulfur bacteria can synthesize all the metabolites, proteins, carbohydrates, and fats of their cells, directly from inorganic materials. What's more, some sulfate reducing bacteria are grown in a vacuum. (53)

Even more pertinent to the situation on Venus, blue-green algae do not depend on solar energy for photosynthesis. They obtain energy from carbon dioxide, which is very abundant on Venus. And these same algae are found living in hot springs at 60°C and in frozen lakes in Antarctica. (54) If these basic life forms have adapted themselves to such harsh conditions, it is at all probable that Venusian life forms would have done the sane, to suit their own conditions, which are mild compared to those cited above.

Even supposing the worst, that the surface temperature of Venus is hot enough to boil away all the water (which seems unlikely), life can exist in the high altitude clouds where the temperature would be lower, but where liquid water is prevalent. Dr. Heinz Haber of the University of California says that Venus "may include a teeming 'biological aerosol' of plankton-like microorganisms upon which flitting creatures feed, perhaps to be eaten by larger things than themselves." (55) However, this may be going a bit too far!

But so far I have been assuming the most adverse conditions. Probably Venus is not as harsh as all that. The dense cloud layer, which does not begin until forty miles above the surface and upon which all speculation of Venusian atmosphere has been based, hides the real atmosphere which living organisms would be utilizing. This portion of the atmosphere is probably clear, or containing elements more favorable to Terran, and thus universal, forms of life, possibly with a surface enshrouded with a lush jungle similar to Terra in Cambrian times. Indeed, to a spectroscope on Venus, Terra may look bone-dry and unsuitable for life, because of our own cloud layer. (56)

By now, life on Venus should be fairly well evolved, representing many forms specifically adapted to its environment. Certainly microorganisms must have populated the oceans and advanced upon the land. Once upon the land, bacteria could "fix" the soil; that is, wear down the rocks and fill it with nitrates. There, their own dead bodies would serve to further the condition of the soil. Then, the microorganisms that live on dead matter, and cause decay, would follow. It is probable that life would have advanced all the way to the form of insects. The wide diversification of insect life is far too large a subject to even open. Already, biologists and taxonomists have classified half a million insects, leaving another half a million which have not even been named yet. These insects survive under any kind of imaginable condition, and have a high mutability factor, making them adaptable to almost anything. Some insects and their close relatives, the spiders (notably, tarantulas), when subjected to simulated Martian conditions, consisting of "thin atmosphere of nitrogen (97%), and only traces of oxygen, carbon dioxide, and argon, with the coldness, dryness, and the lessening effect of gravity, thrived in this almost oxygenless atmosphere. (57)

Above this point life forms become very specialized to one certain, prevailing, and favorable condition, thus reducing its adaptability. If conditions on Venus are too far divergent from those of our own planet, it would be unlikely for life to advance far beyond the insect stage. Of course, assuming a slightly higher temperature (which causes genetic mutations) and the more intense solar radiation level, we must agree that with the increased possibility of mutation, the lines of evolution should have ample time to progress. This leads on to believe that life on Venus should have surpassed life on Terra – not to a point of intelligent life, but to *more* intelligent life!

Man wants to find intelligent life in the universe; someone with whom to trade secrets, to exchange knowledge, and to find companionship. For man has forever been plagued with the prospect of being alone in the universe. And out of this aloneness he has struck out to explore the planets for signs of intelligent life, speculated upon its possibilities, and perhaps cheated a bit in order to swing the cruel facts over to his point of view, a dangerous thing to do. However, in this instance, he will have to search elsewhere than Venus for this long-sought companionship, although he would have been much happier to have found it so near.

The conditions are too variable, and possibly difficult to adapt to. If the most optimum conditions are assumed for Venus, still relying on an essence of the truth, the probability of intelligent life living there is slim – next to impossible. Even if the conditions were exact, convergence, or evolutionary parallelism due to the similarity of conditions and need, stretched as far apart as planets, tends to become stringent. There are too many minor details which are dependent upon existence, and a highly organized system, comparable to a human being, tends to assume a constancy in living conditions. Nature, so strong and enforceful, may have met its better on Venus.

However, there is one thing in the favor of nature eventually evolving into intelligence. "Our whole experience reveals that nature is constantly striving. If evolution is blocked in one direction, it breaks out in another; it is never beaten back." (58) There is hope.

FOOTNOTES

1) George Gaylord Simpson, *The Meaning of Evolution*, p. 125.
2) George Gamow, *Biography of the Earth*, pp 95-97 and p 155.
3) Isaac Asimov, *The Intelligent Man's Guide to the Biological Sciences*, pp 154-156.
4) Harold Spence Jones, *Is There Life on Other Worlds?*, p 146.
5) Spencer, p 146.
6) Willy Ley, *Watchers of the Sky*, p 499.
7) J.H. Rush, *The Dawn of Life*, pp 207-208.
8) Rush, pp 89-90.
9) Charles Darwin, *The Origin of Species*.
10) Kolcum, E.H., "Mariner Reveals 800°F Venus Temperature."
11) H. Spencer Jones, *Life on Other Worlds*, pp 104-105.
12) Jones, p 105.
13) "Cold Clouds Over Venus."
14) Fred L. Whipple, *Earth, Moon, and Planets*, p 204.
15) Martin Gerard Ruttin, *The Geological Aspects of the Origin of Life on Earth*, p 20.
16) Gamow, p 63.
17) Ruttin, p 20.
18) Clifford D. Simak, *The Solar System*, pp 161-162.
19) "Venus Uncovered, Question of Venusian Life."
20) Isaac Asimov, *The Intelligent Man's Guide to the Physical Sciences*, p 145.
21) "Find Nitrogentetroxide in Atmosphere of Venus."
22) V. M. Blanco and S. W. McCuskey, *Basic Physics of the Solar System*, p 61.
23) National Research Council, *The Atmospheres of Mars and Venus*, p 39.
24) Patrick Moore, *The Planet Venus*, p 61.
25) V. A. Firsoff, *Life Beyond the Earth*, p 168.
26) Fred Hoyle, *Frontiers of Astronomy*, p 69.
27) Ernst J. Opik, *The Oscillating Universe*, p 61.
28) Michael W. Ovenden, *Life in the Universe*, p 61.

29) Asimov, *Physical Sciences.*
30) Bernhard, Bennett, Rice, *New Handbook of the Heavens*, p 55.
31) Kolcum.
32) J. H. Peddington, *Radio Astronomy*, pp 108-109.
33) "Venus Uncovered, Question of Venusian Life."
34) Peddington, pp 108-109.
35) Gamow.
36) Jones, pp 102-103.
37) NRC, p 41.
38) NRC, p 43.
39) Patrick Moore, *The Planets*, pp 52-53.
40) NRC, p 46.
41) H. E. Butler, *Atlas of the Universe*, p 224.
42) L. V. Berkner and Hugh Odishaw, *Science in Space*, p 208.
43) Robert Jastrow, Ed., p 142.
44) Rush, p 217.
45) Hoyle, p 73.
46) Opik, p 18.
47) Asimov, *Biological Sciences*, p 162.
48) Patrick Moore and Francis Jackson, *Life in the Universe*, pp 94-95.
49) Moore and Jackson, p 95.
50) Kenneth William Gatland and Derek D. Dempster, *The Inhabited Universe*, p 66.
51) Gatland and Dempster, p 44.
52) Gatland and Dempster, p 44-45.
53) Gatland and Dempster, p 42.
54) Gatland and Dempster, p 43.
55) John W. Macvey, *Life on Other Planets*, p 84.
56) "Life May Exist on Venus."
57) "This is Living."
58) Gatland and Dempster, p 163.

BIBLIOGRAPHY

1) Asimov, Isaac. *The Intelligent Man's Guide to the Biological Sciences*. New York: Pocket Books, Inc., 1960.

2) Asimov, Isaac. *The Intelligent Man's Guide to the Physical Sciences*. New York: Pocket Books, Inc., 1960.

3) Bernhard, Bennett, Rice. *New Handbook of the Heavens*. New York: The New American Library of World Literature, Inc., 1941.

4) V. M. Blanco and S. W. McCuskey. *Basic Physics of the Solar System*. Reading, Massachusetts: Addison-Wesley Publishing Co., Inc., 1961.

5) Butler, H. E. *Atlas of the Universe*. New York: Thomas Nelson and Sons, 1961.

6) "Cold Clouds Over Venus," Science News Letter. (March 9, 1961) 83:149.

7) Darwin, Charles. *The Origin of Species by Means of Natural Selection, or the Preservation of Favored Races in the Struggle for Life*. New York: The New American Library of World Literature, Inc., 1859.

8) "Find Nitrogentetroxide in the Atmosphere of Venus," Science News Letter. (November 14, 1959) 76:319.

9) Firsoff, V. A. *Life Beyond the Earth*. New York: Basic Books, 1963.

10) Gamow, George. *Biography of the Earth*. New York: The New American Library of World Literature, 1941.

11) Hoyle, Fred. *Frontiers of Astronomy*. New York: The New American Library of World Literature, 1955.

12) Jastrow, Robert, Ed. *The Exploration of Space*. New York, The Macmillan Co., 1960.

13) Jones, H. Spencer. *Life on Other Worlds*. The New American Library of World Literature, 1949.

14) Ley, Willy. *Watchers of the Skies*. New York: The Viking Press, 1963.

15) "Life May Exist on Venus." Science Digest. June, 1952. 31:85.

16) Macvey, John W. *Alone in the Universe*. New York: Macmillan, 1963.
17) "Mariner Reveals 800°F Venus Temperature" (E. H. Kolcum) Aviation. March 4, 1963. 78:30-1.
18) Moore, Patrick. *The Planets*. New York: W. W. Norton and Co., Inc., 1962.
19) Moore, Patrick. *The Planet Venus*. New York: Macmillan, 1960.
20) Moore, Patrick and Francis Jackson. *Life in the Universe*. New York: W. W. Norton and Company, Inc., 1962.
21) National Research Council, Science Space Board. Ad Hoc Panel on Planetary Atmospheres. *The Atmospheres of Mars and Venus*. Washington, D.C., National Academy of Sciences, National Research Council, 1961.
22) Odishaw, Hugh and L. V. Barkner. *Science in Space*. New York: McGraw-Hill Book Co., Inc., 1961.

UNTITLED
(THE OTHER WORLD)

I don't remember when I first started noticing it.

It wasn't something that happened overnight, or began all of a sudden.

In fact, it must be months since it originated, coming to my attention gradually as the effects became increasingly more noticeable, daily growing bolder and more striking. Eventually it even affected my mind, which is not, under the circumstances, difficult to understand.

One thing of which I am certain is that it must have started after the unusual lightning storm last summer.

Not that lightning storms are rare enough to be used as a calendar of events. On the contrary, thunderstorms are quite common, and are usually accompanied by magnificent displays of lightning. The location of my house, high on the crest of a hill, overlooking most of the valley and the nearby town, probably attributes to why it experiences more of these pyrotechnic displays than is common to the area.

Of course, I have always felt that there must be a magnetic anomaly which contributes to the abundance of lightning on the hill. It's almost as if the hill were a giant lodestone which attracted lightning whenever a storm was brewing, for it always strikes in the vicinity of the house. That was why Uncle Gaston had embedded so many lightning rods throughout the house and the nearby grounds.

Even before the house was built, Hobbs Hill was known by the local inhabitants to give tremendous shows of color and flashes of lightning during storms.

In fact, the hill was thought to have been haunted.

But Uncle Gaston was not one to be dissuaded in his desires by local hogwash. He believed that everything had a natural explanation, and if Hobbs Hill was struck by lightning more often than the surrounding countryside, it must be because of something in the earth, rather that something that was not of this Earth.

When I first inherited the rambling mansion from Uncle Gaston, I was inclined to sell it and travel across the world on the proceeds of the sale. But his estate was long held in contention because Uncle Gaston did not actually die – he disappeared. I could not legally obtain ownership of the estate until his body was found and the cause of death ascertained.

Instead, I had to move into the mansion and maintain it for the day when Uncle Gaston was declared legally dead, and Hobbs Hill would become mine. The bank allowed me enough money from the estate to live there comfortably, as long as I resided on the premises and kept the house and grounds in good repair. The will even provided enough money for a caretaker. Or caretakers, as the case may be, for I could never induce anyone to live in, and usually they quit after several months. The fact that the place was thought to be haunted contributed to the difficulty in keeping servants.

It was even said that animals never visited the hill. This I found to be untrue, for they often invaded the house.

How long did I have to live in this godforsaken place? Seven years, my lawyers told me, until Uncle Gaston could be declared legally dead. At first I thought it would be an eternity, and I dreaded each passing day of my life. For company I bought a cat and named her Eleanor.

Eventually the house began to grow on me. I became more introverted as time passed, and even learned to enjoy my solitude. I took to reading and writing, and traveled vicariously through literature. And of course, there was endless tinkering to be done to keep the house in repair. There was always paint to be applied, or plaster to be patched, or rotted wood to be replaced. Lights were always going out. Drain pipes were always backing up. Storms blew shingles off the roof, and water made a habit of finding new and ingenious routes into the rooms, often dripping onto the furniture and staining the wallpaper. They sure don't build houses like they used to. Thank God!

Being secluded as it was, and set back in the woods, the house was constantly being invaded by small denizens of the outdoors. Keeping the mice out of the basement and the spider webs from the corners was almost a full time occupation. Especially in winter, the mansion became a refuge for all sorts of undesirable creatures. At first I used to set traps for the mice, and use poison food for the spiders and the myriad other insects. But I never seemed to be able to catch anything, and the poisoned food always went untouched. Yet the sheer numbers of invaders precluded that sometime I should catch something.

Then came the storm. I had been living in the mansion for nearly a year, and was quite used to the dazzling exhibitions as thunderbolts flashed around the grounds and crawled up the copper rods. I would sit on the portico for hours watching the wind-blown trees and the rain-swept grass recoiling under nature's onslaught.

This particular night was worse than any other that I can remember. Flashes of lightning seemed to encircle the entire house, coursing along the ground in a way that was completely unnatural. There was so much static electricity in the air that I could feel my skin crawl. The bright, bluish flashes in the black sky left impressions on my eyes which lasted for several seconds after the bolt had struck. I could well understand why the townspeople avoided Hobbs Hill at any cost.

It was some time later that I began to see things, or rather, to not see things. At first it was only a shadow out of the corner of my eye. When I turned my head it was gone. In a huge dark mansion this was not unusual, for there were many corners where illumination was insufficient. I shrugged it off.

After a while it began to bother me, so that I had to switch on the lights brighter than I had bean used to doing. It wasn't that I was afraid, for I wasn't. But it bothered me always thinking that there was something there, some indefinite quantity which I could not identify.

As I walked past the pantry door I saw a spider on the wall. I stopped to swipe it off, but it ran away. Then a fly dashed in front of my face. I caught only a glimpse of it, but I swung wildly and missed. The odd thing was that it never buzzed, nor was I able to find it again.

The roaches in the basement were becoming bold, for as soon as I walked downstairs they scurried for the corners and disappeared into the cracks and crevices. I never could quite see them, they were so fast. But I knew that they were there. And if I sneaked silently into a room, they somehow knew that I was coming and hid just before I could see them clearly.

I began to get paranoid about the situation, for there seemed to be a clandestine army of mites inhabiting my abode, always one step ahead of me, or just out of sight beyond my range of vision. As soon as I entered a room they would scamper away, leaving without a trace. I began to wonder if they were really there at all, or if I was imagining them.

"It's your eyes," said Mrs. Collins, the old housekeeper who came in once a week to bring my groceries and tidy up a bit. "I used to have the same trouble. Then I went to see Dr. Bebout and he told me I needed spectacles and when I got them I could see so much clearer I never took them off again. If I were you I'd go and see Dr. Bebout. He'll fix you right up, and won't charge you much neither.

I thanked her for her advice, but I could not believe that my problem lay in the need for prescription lenses. No, the insects were really there. They were just too fast for me to catch any more than a glimpse of them.

So I went around the house with all the bulbs lit. I strung extension cords and drop lights throughout the hallways, to illuminate the dark corners and shaded corridors, wherever the bugs could hide. It became a mania with me. I was constantly seeing things on the wall out of the corner of my eye. But when I looked directly at them – they were not there. And there was nowhere that they could have gone. I began to think that I was going mad.

It was easier to believe that my eyesight was failing. Still, I could not go on believing that I was seeing things. In the end I took Mrs. Collins' advice and made an appointment with the local ophthalmologist. I found that Dr. Bebout had died about ten years before, but his very able and highly acclaimed assistant, who had taken over his practice, was willing to examine me.

It was a rare occasion when I left the mansion. I had long since sold my car. A cab picked me up one morning and took me to Dr. Hadley's office.

The doctor was all smiles, going out of his way to make me feel at ease. After he asked a hundred questions about my entire medical history, I finally got to explain my problem to him. He nodded reassuringly as I related my symptoms, occasionally writing pertinent items in his notebook. Then came the tests.

He looked into my eyes with a hundred different instruments. He shone lights on my pupils to test my dilation reflexes. He had me recite letters from a chart on the wall. He had me read from a book through a pair of red glasses, while three-dimensional figures leaped out at me. He checked for color aberrations by asking me to look for hidden numbers on pages of colored dots. He squirted a fluid into my eyes and then tested my eye pressure.

He found my blind spots, and told me that I was right eye dominant. With my chin crushed onto a clamp, he flipped lenses in front of my eyes until I wasn't sure if I was going blind or not. He even took my blood pressure.

"There is nothing wrong with your eyes, Mr. Devonshire. You have perfect twenty-twenty vision, good color distinction, and excellent reaction to luminosity changes. If you take care of your eyes, I would say that they will give you many more years of untroubled use."

"But what about these things that I keep seeing, things moving away just as I look at them? Surely that's not normal?"

"We have things in our eyes called blebs, or floaters, Mr. Devonshire. We are born with them. They are slight imperfections of the eyes when they are formed in the fetus. They usually appear as dots or hairs moving across our eyes. And they are really there. But they are inside the eye, on the cornea, which is why they never come into focus. I would say that you are straining your eyes too much, that you are looking too hard. Try to get a little more sleep and I'm sure you will notice a difference."

I must admit that I felt a little more confident after my visit with Dr. Hadley, for he showed me illustrations from his college textbook which backed up his statements. I vowed thereafter not to notice the little things which were just outside the range of my vision.

Nonetheless, I still kept seeing them. My vision seemed to be worse now that I was aware of the real cause. Into some of the darker rooms of the mansion, which were normally sealed off and unused, and therefore dusty, I extended my ventures. It was really a huge place, and for all its relative newness it was surprisingly old fashioned and mysterious. I even discovered secret panels which revealed storage spaces behind pictures, and walls behind bookcases which were not finished. None of them led anywhere, but I think that Uncle Gaston was planning something for the future.

There were numerous webs in the south wing, more than I would have believed possible. They strung across the room like the drapes of a cathedral, billowing slightly in the breeze of the opening door. I studied them for signs of life, but they all seemed to be devoid of spiders.

Then, out of the corner of my eye, I caught a glimpse of something moving. When I turned my head to look, it was gone. I was frightened at first, but repeated over and over to myself Dr. Hadley's speech. I told myself that there was not really anything there, that I was seeing shapes that drifted across my cornea.

About level with my eyes, for the briefest instant I thought I saw a huge spider clinging to the wall. It wasn't there, naturally, but I still was afraid. In order to break myself of the fear once and for all, I drummed up enough courage to reach out and touch the spot where I thought the phantom existed. Hesitantly I laid my hand against the bright wallpaper, expecting to feel its coolness.

But there was something there! It was big and fluffy, and had many legs which convulsed under by grasp and ran out from under my hand. I screamed and jumped back, tripping over a stool and landing heavily on the floor.

I lay there gasping for several minutes, afraid to move, while my heart raced madly. Still I saw nothing, unless I turned away – and then I might see movement out of the corner of my eye.

Now my imagination ran rampant. I imagined creatures running everywhere across the floor, but when I looked, there was no evidence that anything had moved.

I spotted roaches approaching me in their jerky gait, or disappearing under the furniture. Should I believe Dr. Hadley's explanation? How then to explain the feel of a spider on the wall? Was I possibly becoming over-imaginative because of my seclusion within the mansion? Was my paranoia becoming worse?

Something ran up my leg, under my pants. I screamed and jumped to my feet, shaking the little creature out of my clothing. I felt the soft, furry body against the skin of my leg. I finally dislodged it from my pants and it dropped to the floor. For the barest instant I saw a little mouse. Then it was gone like the rest of the phantoms of my mind. It did not run away, I am certain – I simply could not see it. It was as if the mouse had become suddenly invisible.

I ran screaming from the room, remembering in my haste to slam the door behind me, lest any of the foul creatures escape into the rest of the mansion. I ran though the house until I reached the well-lighted kitchen where I believed that the bright lights would protect me from the inner reaches of my mind – if these creatures truly existed only in my mind.

Perhaps it was time for me to see a psychiatrist. I was certain now that my problem was more than optical, for the quasi-invisible creatures actually existed. But if they really existed, I needed an exterminator rather than a psychiatrist. I could no longer be certain of anything. Are the creatures real or aren't they? Are they in my mind or my imagination? Are my eyes going bad, or am I being affected by my lonely existence in the mansion?

I sat in the middle of the kitchen table and pulled my legs up from the edge. *They* were down there on the floor. I could almost see them, out of the corner of my eye, scurrying about. A big cockroach seemed to peer out from under the refrigerator, but was gone when I looked at it. I caught a glimpse of mouse running across the threshold of the dining room. A hairy spider reposed silently on the ceiling above me, ready to drop on me and wrap its hairy legs around my head. Other critters were indiscernible.

These creatures really existed. I could almost see them!

I jumped to the floor and dashed up the stairs to my bedroom – my last refuge – where I leaped onto my bed and drew myself under the covers. I sobbed and sobbed, hiding like an ostrich, hoping that the creatures would not see me. They were all around me. And whenever I ran my eyes across the room I would nearly see half a dozen of them, scurrying about. Finally, my tremors induced exhaustion, and I fell into a troubled sleep.

When I awoke it was morning, and the sun was streaming into the windows. My fears of the night before were practically gone. I felt for certain that I had dreamt the whole episode.

Eleanor padded warily into the room. At least I

thought she did. When I looked on the floor, the cat had vanished. I wonder what she thought of my strange actions.

A small shape dashed across the floor. I thought it was a mouse, but when I looked directly at it, there was nothing there. Then a larger shape caught my eye. For a moment I thought it was the cat, but my delusions of the night before must still have been afflicting me. I definitely heard a crash as the night stand tumbled to the floor, and the expensive china shattered when it hit the bare boards.

Startled, I looked for an explanation. Again I thought I saw the cat, but when I looked hard, she was not there. Cats are pretty elusive, especially when they do things wrong, so I was not too surprised. Yet after the experiences of the night before, I was wary.

I looked around the room for Eleanor, but saw nothing. Then there was a sudden lurch on the bed, and I caught a glimpse of Eleanor jumping onto the sheets behind me. I turned around to pull her close to me – but she was not there. Still, I had heard and felt something. My fear began to come back to me.

Something furry brushed by my face. I jumped and screamed, practically throwing the bed sheets onto the floor. I saw the cat race out of the room. The damned cat had really given me a fright, sneaking around like that.

As I strolled through the long dark hallways to the kitchen, I heard Eleanor meow faintly, as if she were a long way off. Then I saw her standing on the landing at the top of the stairs, but just for at instant, for then she vanished, as cats are wont to do. I heard her patter down the steps, and stop about halfway down. Yet when I stared down the staircase, I saw no sign of her. Was she crouching beneath a riser?

Again I heard the far off cry, appearing to come from somewhere in front of me. I worked my way down the stairs. Something furry brushed my legs, and when I looked down there was the cat – but then she was gone.

I stood in abject fear. I heard the faraway cry. Fearfully, I reached down and stroked the spot where I thought I had seen her. And she was there! I could feel her, and faintly hear her, and when I turned and looked away I could almost see her out of the corner of my eye. She was there, but she appeared to be fading out of existence the way the smaller creatures had gone before her.

Eleanor pattered down the stairs to the landing, and disappeared from my sight forever.

*   *   *   *   *

The next time Mrs. Collins came to do the housework, I followed her around and told her my story. She glanced past me occasionally, as if to acknowledge my presence, but otherwise she took no notice of me, and never did she make any comment.

Now you can understand why I acted so strangely the last time you were here, Mrs. Collins. I actually thought that I was going crazy. But now I know that the mansion is truly haunted. Not in the conventional way, of course, but haunted just the same.

Not that you would notice anything right away. But it seems to grow on you. After you live here for a while, you begin to see the things that are normally not visible to the human eye. You see the insects and spiders and mice out of the corner of your eye, almost seeing them in full, but not quite. You're never really certain if they are really there, or if they are just a figment of your vivid imagination.

The explanation is not to be found within your mind. You see, the strange magnetic qualities of this hill, and therefore the house, affect living tissue. It works on them until they eventually fade away from this world. After a while you begin to fade into the other world also, and you can see more and more clearly into it. The things you see out of the corner of your eye are little insights into this other world, and when they become bolder and bolder, you know that you are slipping away too.

Of course, it takes time. The smaller creatures fade away first, living in this other world just as well as they lived in ours. But the affect is cumulative, and the more time you spend in this house, the more you are absorbed into the other world. And the closer you get to it, the more you can see into it, until eventually you fade from this world altogether. Then you begin to have trouble seeing into this world, the real world.

It's quite a relief, Mrs. Collins, realizing the truth, and understanding the scientific basis. For a while I thought that I was seeing creatures that didn't exist. But now I know that those creatures actually do exist, only in a different plane of existence. Eventually, the bigger creatures slip into the other world. Larger masses take longer to make the transition.

No. Don't go, Mrs. Collins. I'm not finished yet. You see, size makes a difference. It takes longer for a cat to slip away than, for instance, a mouse.

And it takes longer for a mouse than for a spider or a cockroach. The little ones go first, but the big ones are not far behind. If a person remains within the influence of this house long enough, even they start to disappear. They fade into the other world, just like Uncle Gaston must have done.

So you see, it wasn't my eyes at all. Dr. Hadley's theories were all hogwash. I was seeing things that were on the verge of fading from sight and becoming part of another existence. That's why I want to leave with you today and get away from this house forever.

Because soon this anomaly is going to affect me as it did the others. Just like eventually it affected Eleanor, and Uncle Gaston. If I don't leave now, the force is going to take me into that other world, which must be overly populated with spiders and roaches and mice. I don't want to go to that world, Mrs. Collins.

You're not paying attention to me, Mrs. Collins. I'm not crazy, believe me. It's the house that's crazy, and the sooner I get away from it the safer I will be. Mrs. Collins, listen to me.

What do you mean, where am I? I'm standing right here in front of you. Don't go searching the house, Mrs. Collins. I'm right here. What? I told you, I didn't go anywhere. But I want to go back to town with you. I'll get a hotel room or something until I can settle things with the bank. But I can't afford to stay here any longer.

Mrs. Collins, please listen to me. I've got to leave with you. I promise you I'm not insane. I won't cause you any trouble, believe me. I'll be very quiet, just please take me with you. You can even take me to the hospital if you like. I don't care, just as long as you get me away from this house.

Mrs. Collins. Wait for me. I want to go with you. Mrs. Collins, listen to me. Mrs. Collins. I'm here, standing right in front of you. Mrs. Collins, don't leave without me. You must understand. You must believe me. Don't leave me.

Mrs. Collins, Please don't go. Mrs. Collins. Don't go. The house will take me away if you go without me. Mrs. Collins. Mrs. Collins. Don't go. Don't go.

Don't go away!

*   *   *   *   *

I spent fruitless hours in the cellar, searching and calling, although I knew that it was fruitless. Eleanor, like the countless creatures before her, had left this world forever. If I ever saw her again it would be only for the fleetest instant, for the briefest moment of time, as one plane of hers became visible.

Whether the house has anything to do with this strange phenomenon, or if it is due to the unusual qualities of Hobbs Hill, I cannot be sure. The line between reality here and reality there is very thin. Only a sharp mind can perceive the difference. Eleanor's disappearance was the penultimate test.

And so my theory needs but one more proof.

I have seen how the smaller creatures of God's world were the first to succumb to the power of change. After a while the larger animals such as mice and rats and birds, under the strange influence, faded into that other world. In time, Eleanor, having spent so long in the house with me, suffered the same fate.

She has entered that other reality which must certainly be over-populated with insects and spiders and ugly mites. And the closer one gets to that world, the more one can see into it.

I know that I am repeating myself, but I can't help it.

The things which one thinks one sees out of the corner of one's eye become bolder and more pronounced. It is the first sign that one is slipping away. And if one is not careful, one will slip away forever, into that insect-filled world.

Already I can feel the effects of the power, for I can see into that world more clearly. I can see creepy and crawly things all around me. They make me sick. I try to withdraw from them, but I am quickly losing my grasp on reality.

Already I am losing my grip. The cellar stairs have dissolved under my feet. I try to climb them, but they have faded from under me, trapping me in the cellar. I try to reach the landing, but when I jump, the floor falls away from me.

I have to get out of this world before it engulfs me. They are all around me now. I can see them. They are on the walls and the ceiling and crawling on the floor. I don't like it here, and I have to get out. I have to get out of the cellar.

I don't want to trade realities. I don't want to live in a world that is inhabited solely by insects and mice and rats. I want to go home.

The stairs have faded away. I can only sit in the corner, warding off the insects by drawing my knees close to my chest. I put my hand in my mouth to prevent myself from screaming.

Somebody has to come and get me, to drop a ladder from the landing so I can climb out of here. Quickly, before the door fades too, for then it will be too late. Someone has to help me.

I'm fading from this world, retreating into an unpleasant otherness. I can only hold on to this reality for so long. Someone help me. I'm disappearing. Someone help me. I'm fading.

Help me. . . . Help me. . . . Help me.   Help me. . . Help me. . . .
Help me. . . . Help me. . . . Help me . . . Help me . . .

The Eyes of the Beholder

Bill Sanders' eyes opened slowly, turning the dark visions that were painted on the inside of his eyelids to vague but brighter mists. Dim and fuzzy shapes moved among those mists, crossing back and forth with a feeling of depth. It was like watching clouds at different altitudes blowing in different directions. More than that he could not perceive. His eyes closed to a more tangible reality.

He heard the word "Marion."

Later, when his eyes opened again, the clouds acquired definition as they took on fantastic, other-worldly shapes: a night stand with a glass of water resting on it, a chair made of plain wood, a closed door, a computer console with flashing lights, and life-recording telemetering displays. He recognized the latter, and it helped to dispel somewhat his disorientation.

He was in a hospital.

A shadow moved toward him, into the light, and coalesced into the shape of a man: short mousy face, pinched nose, squinting gray eyes behind thick horn-rimmed lenses, wire-thin mustache, white uniform. He became aware of pressure on his arm.

"How do you feel, Bill?" the mousy man asked, smiling.

"Who? . . . What? . . . "

"The classic question is 'where am I?' " the man said, still smiling. He revealed two even rows of white teeth – friendly teeth.

"Where – Where am I?" Sanders stuttered, as if in a voice that was speaking for the first time.

"Hopkins Medical Center," the man said. When Sanders made no sign of recognition, he continued.

"You've had an accident. Do you remember?"

After a long pause, during which the room was surfeited with silent longing, he said, "No."

"Do you know who I am?"

Again, a long pause. "No."

"Do you know who *you* are?"

Another pause, with squinting eyes. "No."

"Can you remember anything?"

"No."

"Go back to sleep. We'll talk again later."

Bill Sanders slept.

When he next awoke the room was fully lighted. The mousy man was sitting alongside him. Behind him stood another man: tall, crew cut, sharp features, penetrating eyes of amethyst, muscular, white uniform.

"How are you feeling, Bill?" the mousy man asked.

No pause. "Fine."

"Do you remember where you are?"

"A hospital,"

"Do you remember *who* you are?"

"Bill."

"Good. You're learning fast. Do you know who *I* am?"

"A doctor."

"That too. You're deductive reasoning is returning. But I'm also your friend and associate, George Murdock." Bill Sanders nodded ever so faintly.

"Do you know who this is?" Murdock asked, indicating the man standing behind him.

Blank.

"This is Don Jenkins."

"Hi, Bill. Glad to have you back," said the muscular man named Jenkins, matter-of-factly. There was no sense of humor in his demeanor.

No question was asked, so Bill did not answer.

"Do you remember him?" Murdock asked, with his ever-present smile.

"No."

"And you still don't remember the accident?"

"No."

"Traumatic memory loss," Jenkins said clinically.

Murdock shook his head. "Can you remember anything at all – from before?"

A long pause. Before he could answer, Jenkins said, "Give him time, George. Don't rush him."

Murdock was testy. "Don't rush to any conclusions yourself."

"Only opinions are rushed. Conclusions are merely based upon available data."

"Then wait until you have some data."

Jenkins' face was getting red. "Loss of memory is indicative in itself."

"It is indicative that the drug did more than it was supposed to do."

"Goddamn it, George. It's only amnesia as a result of the accident." Jenkins stopped staring at the man in the bed, and walked across the room as if to terminate the discussion.

"But there was no concussion," Murdock said. He spun around and scanned the digital readings on the display screen. "Tell me, Bill, do you feel any pain? Any pain at all?" He aimed his kindly face at Sanders as he spoke.

"No."

"Well, your drug seems to be doing *something* good, in any case."

Jenkins stalked back and fairly exploded. "It's not the drug, I'm telling you. He must still be in shock, that's all."

"Don, if you were a pathologist instead of a research biochemist you'd know that the computer shows no sign of shock, nor of any other metabolic disorder or neurological dysfunction. And since there was no damage to the brain, the only affordable conclusion is that, while he maintains an excellent state of physical health, his brain is blocked from all but involuntary functions."

"He can talk, can't he?" Jenkins snapped, walking back and peering into Sanders' eyes. "Can't you?"

Bill Sanders stared blankly.

"Stop it, Don, and act your age. Don't go taking it out on him. You're the one who gave him an untested drug."

"I told you that he wanted me to."

"And do you normally give your patients whatever they ask for?"

"Come on, George, you know it's the chance we've been waiting for. Sure, if we had had the authority to try it out on another patient, a terminally ill, a hopelessly insane – "

"I'm not going to argue with you about it now," Murdock said, his friendly smile disappearing into a wry contortion. "Those decisions are not up to me alone to make. I'm not the whole medical examining board, just one doctor who sits on it."

"You're the chief resident surgeon, not a family doctor. You throw around a lot of weight, not only in this hospital, but in the State. You could have influenced the board, if you had tried."

"You know my reasons. I felt there was not enough experimental data."

"How many mice do we have to stab before we know it's safe? We've been testing for two years, and we've shown conclusively that the drug stops pain as completely as if it didn't exist, and that the relief from pain induces chemical changes that accelerate the healing process. We've had dozens of mice with artificially broken limbs get up and dart about their cage within a week."

"But a mouse can't tell you what it's feeling," Murdock persisted. "Or thinking."

"And that's precisely why we needed a human subject. It just so happened that Bill was the one."

"And now he can't even remember his own name."

For the first time during the argument, Bill Sanders registered interest. Slowly, almost childishly, he said, "My name is Bill."

Murdock and Jenkins returned their attention to Sanders.

Murdock leaned forward and said, "Bill what?" He

sounded calm, but had not succeeded in getting the smile back on his face.

Sanders stared back at him blankly. "Bill . . . Bill . . ."

"Maybe he needs something to jostle his memory," Jenkins said harshly. "Or someone."

Murdock shook his head.

"Well, at least let me bring her in."

"It's for her sake that I left her out," Murdock said.

"Then how about for *his* sake we let her in?"

Murdock did not answer. Neither did he resist.

"All right," Jenkins continued. "I'll be right back."

When he had left the room and the two of them were alone, Murdock practiced his best bedside manner, and conducted a thorough examination. The Medwife stood by him all the time, never leaving his side for a moment. The computer could give decimal place accuracies on blood pressure, pulse rate, breathing rate, and other signs of vital functions, but it could not feel with experienced hands. Methodically, he went over Bill Sanders' injuries.

The left foot had been badly smashed, and the bones had been splintered. The cast began just below the knee and extended all the way to the toes, which were open to allow airflow, but which were splinted so there was no possibility of movement. Murdock pinched the toes.

"Do you feel any pain, Bill?"

Sanders was hardly paying attention. "No," he said absently.

Murdock squeezed the right calf just below the traction pin, He had drilled a hole through the shin bone and had inserted a stainless steel pin to which, by a complicated arrangement of pulleys, was attached ten pounds of weight that stretched the broken femur apart in order to force the ends of the bones grow out before knitting. It would prevent leg shrinkage. The leg, other than a support running under it from hip to ankle, was exposed, and showed the long scars where Murdock had opened it up in order to set the bone.

"Do you feel any of this?" Murdock asked, feeling and squeezing all the way along the length of the leg, even over the break.

Weakly, Sanders muttered, "No."

Murdock grimaced, and clucked to himself. The muscles seemed to be strong and firm around the break, helping to hold it together. It had not been a compound fracture, but a simple break. Still, he had been unable to set it and, after three abortive tries, had had to operate in order to get the uneven ends to align. Now, it seemed to be doing well.

Other than several deep cuts, the hip area had essentially escaped damage. Murdock ran his practiced hands over the chest, which had been heavily taped to contain the broken ribs. With one hand on either side, he squeezed gently, listening for the cracking of bone. All was silent. They were meshed properly.

"How do you feel, now?" Murdock said quietly. He had never had a more subdued patient.

"Tired."

"No pain at all?" he said, while pinching the fingers that protruded from the cast on his right arm. They were no longer livid, but appeared warm and pink, a sign of good circulation.

"No," Sanders said drowsily.

"Can you feel this at all?"

"Yes."

"You can feel, but not pain?"

"Yes."

"Amazing." Murdock stepped closer to Sanders' face and peered into the one half-open eye. The pupil was not dilated, and reacted well to light when he shaded it from the overhead light with his hand. The other eye was heavily bandaged, as was the whole side of the face. The nose had been broken, the cheek bone splintered, but the jaw was intact and the head was free of injury. It had been a very lucky accident, if accidents could be said to be lucky. What he meant was that it could have been worse.

With great effort, Sanders roused himself from his

lethargy. "Doctor – Murdock – "

"Call me George."

"George – when can I get up?"

"Not for a long time, I'm afraid. You're very weak, and your injuries will take time to heal."

"No. No. That's nothing. I just feel weak."

"And you should. But you need your rest."

"No. I don't like being tied down,"

"You're not tied down – in that sense. You just need time to recover. But argumentation is good. It shows that your spirit is well."

Still struggling to stay awake, Sanders continued. "I'm already recovered. I just need some energy so I can get out of here."

"Ah, you're accepting too much from the drug. You see, it has completely obliterated any hint of pain, and that is good because it has relieved your mind to concentrate on other things, and has let your body heal without the attendant psychological trauma. But it is bad because without the sensation of pain, you think you are well, and might do yourself an injury by trying to do something that you would ordinarily be prevented from doing because of excruciating pain. You must understand this, accept it intellectually, and remain calm until I tell you that your body has healed, and not start moving around when you feel that it is all right to do so."

Sanders took a deep breath. His strength was leaving him fast, and this last effort was almost too much for him. "I'm all right, I tell you. There's nothing wrong with me other than superficial scars, like this one on my arm. And that will go away if I have energy."

Murdock was silent for a long moment. "Bill, go to sleep now. I will check in later and see that you have a substantial amount of food. It has only been hours since I took you off intravenous feeding. The return of your appetite so soon is certainly a good sign. Now sleep."

Sanders had burned himself out. He wanted to argue, but instead he slept.

Murdock left the room just in time to prevent Don Jenkins from coming in with a similarly white-clad woman: medium height, thin but tight body, firm breasts, strong but feminine features, narrow pink nose, smooth cheeks, shoulder length auburn hair.

"How is he?" she said hesitantly.

"He's asleep. He's been through a lot and he needs his rest."

"Can I see him?"

"In the best interests of all, I think not."

"George, I'm not afraid to see him all bandaged up. After all, I dragged him out of the car myself when he was broken and bloody. He can't look any worse now."

"It's not how he looks that I'm preventing you from seeing. It's how he feels."

"What wrong with the way he feels? Don told me that the drug worked one hundred percent as anticipated, and that he feels no pain whatsoever."

Murdock cast threatening look at Jenkins.

The biochemist returned it just as threateningly.

"Don did not tell you the whole story. The drug has also induced some form of amnesia – how permanent or temporary I don't know."

"The drug didn't do it, I tell you," Jenkins fairly screamed. "That drug has been used on scores of mice and they showed no ill effects."

"But you only tested them for physical defects," Murdock insisted. "Did you think to use trained mice, maze runners, to see if they could remember how to run a maze after they were given the drug?"

"We weren't testing them for psychoses, George, we were testing them for regenerative effects."

"And that's why I, as a member of the board, would not allow your drug to be tested on human beings. People are not test subjects. A drug is always to be considered potentially dangerous until every aspect of it has been tested. You blinded yourself by looking only at the positive effects without acknowledging the possibilities of deleterious side effects. Now we have a man in there who can't remember his own name."

"Please! Please!" Marion pleaded. "I want to know how Bill is. Your arguments can keep until later."

Murdock sighed. "Yes, of course. I'm sorry, Marion."

Jenkins huffed as Murdock continued.

"Physically, Bill is doing fine. He's very weak, as should be expected, but he is responding extraordinarily well to treatment. Unbelievably, his blood count is normal, his sugar level is normal, his fluid level is normal. I've had all the IV's removed – he can get by with an occasional antibiotic injection. And he's ready to drink and eat solid foods. In my opinion he is in about the third week of recovery."

"In only three days," Jenkins added.

"In only three days," Murdock admitted. "But. . . . " And here he hesitated.

Marion looked at him strangely, questioningly. "Come on, George. Stop the melodramatics. I'm not a stereotypic whimpering female – I'm a psychiatric nurse. I handle cases like his every day."

"But you don't have the emotional attachment with your patients that you have with Bill."

"Stop it. Just tell me. I have a right to know,"

"All right. He has almost total amnesia. He can't remember who he is, who I am, who Don is. And I doubt very much that he will remember who you are. You see, I'm not afraid of *him* being hurt by your meeting. I'm afraid of *you* being hurt."

Marion drew in a deep breath. "How is that possible? He had no head injuries."

"That is what I intend to find out," Murdock said. "But I'd rather do it my own way."

"I still want to see him."

Murdock shook his head as he gazed into her forceful, blue eyes. "Let me see him once more, when he wakes up. Then I'll talk it over with you. But for right now, let him sleep. You won't gain anything by a visual inspection. I know you don't want to really 'see' him. You want to converse with him."

A glistening tear crept out of Marion's eye. "It's all my fault . . . "

"Nothing is your fault," Murdock said, taking her in his elderly arms and holding her tight.

Marion refused to cry. Instead, she said to Jenkins. "Don, I don't blame you for anything that has happened. I know that Bill wanted it this way. And if I had been in that car instead of him, I'd be lying in there now . . ."

"Don't even think that," Murdock said.

"But it's true. I put him in that car. I made him angry enough to speed. If I hadn't been so unreasonable, he wouldn't have had that accident – or, at least, he wouldn't have had it alone. But, George, I volunteered to take that drug if anything had happened to me. I believe in the advancement of science, and medicine, just as much as Bill does, and Don does. You were the one being unreasonable by not letting him try it on some of the patients."

"My dear, I'm not going to have this argument again. I've already had it out with Don. For right now, let's forget the recriminations and worry about Bill. Let's accept the situation and take it from there."

"That's the first intelligent thing you've said all day," Jenkins said, glaring at Murdock.

Later, in Bill Sanders' room, George Murdock was sitting by his bed when he opened his eyes.

"Good morning. Sleep well?"

Bill, still in the throws of sleep, nodded imperceptibly.

"Good. Well, how do you feel this morning?"

"Fine, but weak. I don't have any energy."

"You know, you ate enough supper last night to keep an army alive."

"I'm not talking about food. I need energy."

"Well, that will all come with time. You're healing unusually well. I've examined you last night, and I'm amazed at your progress. Bones are already beginning to knit. Your muscle tone is strong. And according to the Medwife, your vital signs are as good as mine – perhaps even better. I'm getting old, you know, and you're still a young man."

Bill Sanders eyed him speculatively, but said nothing.

"You know, you said something yesterday that, well, didn't make an impression on me at the time. The more I thought about it, the more I began to wonder. Tell me, Bill, how did you know there was a scar on your arm?"

"I could see it." His voice was soft and calm, as if it were a very simple question with a very simple answer.

"Oh? And can you see it now?"

Sanders' gaze went down. "Of course."

"And what else can you see on your arm?"

Now Sanders narrowed his eyes, "Just skin."

Murdock pondered this for a moment before continuing. "Can you see the stitches, too?" When Sanders nodded, he said, "How many?"

Sanders counted for several seconds, nodding his head with each number. "Sixteen."

"Very good. Your eyesight is excellent. Much better than it should be, in fact. And you still feel no pain?"

"No."

"Well, what do you feel?"

"Hunger."

Murdock laughed. "Breakfast will be right along."

But Sanders ignored his humor. "Not here," he said, indicating his belly. He moved his hand to the middle of his chest. "Here."

Murdock nodded knowingly, "I have just the thing for you. In fact, she'll be here shortly. But for now, let me look you over."

As before, Dr. George Murdock examined every inch of Bill Sanders' body with his fingers, squeezing and pinching in such a way that ordinarily pain would have been inevitable. But Sanders never flinched. Murdock removed the patch from Sanders' right eye. He observed that it was bloodshot but otherwise normal. Even the swelling around it had gone down. He replaced the patch and added fresh tape.

Murdock looked at Sanders thoughtfully for a moment. Then, retreating to the foot of the bed, he studied the Medwife's display. He nodded to himself, then returned to Sanders' side.

"Against all medical experience, you appear to be the most normal man I've ever seen. Your biostats are probably better than mine. But I want to test your eyesight. Do you mind?"

"No"

"Good." Murdock opened the top button of his hospital gown and removed a common stethoscope. But instead of approaching Sanders with it he walked back to the door. He held it out in front of him, in such a way that it was perpendicular to Sanders' line of sight. "Bill, I want you to tell me which tube is closer to you."

Sanders remained impassive. "They're the same."

"Good." Now, I'm going to turn it so that one side or the other will be closer. Tell me what you see."

As he did, Bill said, "Left. Left. Right. Left. Left. Left. Right. Right."

"Thank you, Bill. I'll be going now, but someone else will be here shortly with your breakfast. Get down all you can, so you can bring up your energy level."

He stepped into the hallway and walked to the end of the corridor, where there was a conference room. Jenkins and Marion were waiting for him there.

"You may go and see him now, Marion," Murdock said. "He's fully awake. Take in the food tray and see that he dines well."

"Thanks, George," she said simply, and left. She tried to mask her features, but the anxiety showed through the façade of equanimity.

"It's about time you let her see him," Jenkins said smugly. "The poor girl's going crazy with worry."

"And Bill's going crazy without it," Murdock retorted. "He is, after all, the primary patient. And that poor girl can handle herself quite well. She's not the weak kitten you're used to dating, Don."

"Let's keep this on a professional basis."

"Ah, you only say that when the argument is going against you. You didn't feel that way yesterday. But no matter, we have more important matters at hand."

Before Jenkins could riposte, Murdock continued. "Don, I can you tell me if your mice ever had any, shall we say, perceptual problems."

"You can't test a mouse for perception – they never answer your questions," he said, trying to get even for Murdock' s astringent remarks.

"Well, perhaps perception is a poor choice of word – at least for a mouse. But, did they have any difficulty with their vision?"

Jenkins reverted back to a biochemist, and said, "None that I could ever see."

"Did they act strange after the injection – in a way that would lead you to believe that they had other than normal vision?"

"No, their eyes appeared to be fine. The only difficulty we had with the mice was keeping them tied down. The absence of pain was so complete that they tried to get up and walk around all the time, despite extensive injuries. Why? Have you noticed something wrong with Bill's eyes?"

"Not something wrong, perhaps, but something odd. You see, he mentioned yesterday that his wounds were superficial, that he was done healing, and that he had only minor cosmetic scars left to heal. He mentioned the scar on his arm. I let it pass, thinking naturally that he could feel the line of incision where I had to open him up to set the bones. But this morning I delved into it more. And you know what? He was able to tell me that he had sixteen stitches on his arm. The exact amount, I might add, that I put in."

Jenkins squinted his eyes. "So."

"Ah, you miss the obvious. You see, there are only two ways that he could know that. Either he has an unusual sensitivity, one which allows him to feel, if you will, each and every stitch – and this I doubt, because of his lack of feeling pain – or he can see through plaster. You forget that he has a cast on that arm."

            *   *   *   *   *

Marion slipped through the door with a steaming breakfast tray in her hands and a ready smile on her face. "Hi," she said nonchalantly.

"Hi," Sanders replied.

"I brought you some food. The doctor says you need to build up your strength."

Sanders eyed her suspiciously.

She put the tray down across his body so that it rested on its legs over his outstretched legs.

Sanders never took his eyes off her.

She returned his gaze. "Bill," she said, then faltered. Taking a deep breath, she plunged right into the heart of the matter. "Bill, do you know who I am?"

"A nurse."

Then she did what she promised herself she would not do. She burst into tears.

Sanders watched her, but remained impassive.

When she finally stopped crying, and had wiped her eyes on a tissue, she attempted to smile. "I'm sorry, Bill. I just didn't think it was true. You really don't know who I am, do you?"

"No," he said, with an attitude that implied that his ignorance did not concern him.

"Don't you know my name?"

Indifferently, he said, "No."

"I'm Marion – Sanders. I'm your wife."

*   *   *   *   *

In the conference room, Murdock was taking a seat as Jenkins realized the import of the statement that he had just made. "What are you trying to pull on me, George? What are you suggesting?"

"I'm suggesting nothing, just pointing out observations. I then took it a step further and performed a simple test for depth perception. He scored a hundred in it, as if he could see with two good eyes. Did I mention that he still had the patch over his eye? Ah, now you begin to catch on, don't you? What I at first thought was a simple case of brain damage is turning into something out of the realm of medical science."

Jenkins huffed. "First of all, the drug does not damage the brain. It numbs the ganglia in the backbone and prevents pain signals from reaching the brain. It's an isolator, that's all."

"It's also an amputator. We're getting into a new area of science. We don't know how the brain reacts to the total absence of stimuli. And certainly, the human brain would react differently than an animal brain because of the higher cognitive functions."

"Which is why I was bucking for human subjects all along," Jenkins added.

"Which is I wouldn't give them to you." Murdock sat back almost as if he were lounging. "However, we have one now. One who can feel sensation, but no pain – which is unexplainable, since both stimuli must reach the brain. If one stimulus reaches the brain, why doesn't the other? That, however, is a scientific quandary, and since it has been introduced against my wishes the question is entirely academic. The real problem is that I have a patient who has amnesia for some unknown reason – I will not attack your drug again.

If Jenkins heard him he made no notice.

"And what is more, he doesn't care that he has amnesia. That is what I can't understand."

*   *   *   *   *

Marion entered the room and sat down heavily in a hardwood chair opposite Murdock. Her head drooped to one side, as if it was all she could do to hold it up.

"Was it that bad?" Murdock asked, in a fatherly manner.

Two tears rolled down her cheeks. "He didn't know who I was."

"I told you – "

"He didn't *care* who I was." She wiped the tears off her face with the back of her hand. "Even after I told him."

Jenkins said, "It's understandable in his present state of mind – "

"It's not his mind, but his brain," said Murdock.

"What's the difference – ?" Marion started to say. But then her long years of training took control of her thinking. She knew the difference between the mind and the brain.

"Give him some time – "

Murdock cut off Jenkins with evident anger. "Time has nothing to do with his condition. The drug has affected his brain, and his brain is now affecting his mind. We need to confront Bill's condition, not make excuses for it." He turned to Marion. "My dear, I tried to keep you away from him before, but now I need you to go back to him. Perhaps your presence can effect some therapeutic cognizance. Will you come with me?"

She wiped away more tears. "Of course, if that is what you think is best." She was not only a nurse who understood Murdock's rationale, but a wife whose love for her husband was willing to clutch at any straw to bring him back from pathologic introversion.

Murdock and Jenkins escorted Marion to Sanders' room.

Sanders' face registered no recognition. He looked alternately at Marion and Murdock and Jenkins.

Marion sat on the edge of Sanders' bed. "Why, Bill? Why?"

Sanders was silent. His silence was more than Marion could bear. She sobbed unabashedly. Jenkins put an arm around her shoulders and lifted her from the bed. He helped her, still sobbing, to the door. She turned and looked back at her husband. Sanders' face was blank. Then Jenkins dragged Marion out of the room, and closed the door behind them.

When the door had closed, Murdock asked, "You really don't remember?"

"I don't understand. What am I supposed to remember?"

"You don't remember me, or Don Jenkins, or your own wife?"

"No."

"Are you even interested in remembering?"

"No."

"I thought as much. You are the strangest case of amnesia I've ever encountered. You show no evidence of curiosity about who you are, or what happened to you, or anything about you. You lie there like some smug vegetable willing to take everything that comes along, but offering nothing to anyone. You're cruel. You're a heartless animal, without a soul."

Sanders stared indifferently.

Murdock swallowed, grasped his arms, and said, "I'm sorry, Bill. I was testing you. It was necessary. Apparently the drug has also dampened your emotional response, as well as your response to pain stimuli. I don't know if that's good or bad. But what is more important, I don't know if its effects will wear off."

Uncaring, Sanders stared blankly.

"You never should have done it. It was too risky. You should have waited until someone was in danger of dying, not just suffering from, well, massive injuries such as you received. Certainly, the pain aspect is proven beyond a question of a doubt, but we don't understand the side effects of the drug."

When Sanders made no reply, Murdock continued, "If your curiosity is not aroused enough to ask any questions, perhaps I should explain enough to try to jar your memory back into place. The accident was a bad one. Your car slid off the road in a rainstorm, and crashed into a tree. You sustained serious injuries, but nothing that was life threatening as long as you received prompt and proper medical care and treatment.

"Your right tibia was broken in two places. Two lumbar transverse processes were broken but no spinal column damage was sustained. You had two fractured ribs, a compound fracture of the ulna, and a crushed cheek and facial muscles, all on the right side."

Sanders nodded noncommittally.

"You were in pain – agonizing pain – mostly from your leg and arm. There was little if any interior hemorrhage, so you were in little serious trouble. But Don Jenkins administered a new, untested pain killer. Instead of working on the nervous system by lowering the brain's threshold to pain, it works directly on the brain, stopping pain – and pleasure for that matter – stopping all tactile stimuli. In a sense, it is the perfect drug. It allows virtually no pain, pleasure, and apparently no emotion, to impinge upon the brain. It seems to have severed the brain completely from the rest of the nervous system. Possibly permanently."

Sanders will still impassive.

"Don't you understand the implication of this? You may never recover your memory, and you don't even care. At least ask me something so I know that you're still a thinking human being, and not some monster devoid of reason."

After a long while, Sanders responded. "How long ago . . . ?"

"Three days."

"No, not since I first regained consciousness. How long ago since the accident?"

"Three days."

For the first time, emotion registered on Sanders' face, although the expression was unreadable. "But that's impossible. I couldn't have healed that fast."

"You aren't healed. You just can't feel any pain."

"But I'm not in any pain. There's nothing wrong with me. I'm well."

"You're not blind, are you? You've got broken bones all up and down your body."

Sanders glanced down at his legs, lying on the bed, then at his arms. His eyes danced with a strangeness that prompted Murdock's next question.

"Tell me, Bill, what do you see?"

"I see . . . I see two legs, two arms. I see hospital pajamas. I see . . . "

Murdock squinted, and peered deeply into Sanders' eyes. He opened the drawer to the nightstand, pulled out a mirror, and held it in front of Sanders' face.

"Tell me what you see."

"Well, I see a face, clean shaven, smooth, hair combed neatly and parted, thin nose – "

Murdock jerked the mirror away and tossed it into the drawer. "That drug has affected your brain more than I thought. It has not only cut off all stimuli of pain or pleasure, and caused amnesia, but it has induced self-delusion. Bill, your face is half covered with bandages, your ribcage is taped, your arm is in a cast, your leg is in traction. And you tell me that you see none of these things?"

"Doctor," Sanders said, for the first time taking the initiative. "You are the one who is deluded. I'm telling you that there is nothing wrong with me. Look. Look at my arm. I can lift it above my head. Could I do that if it were broken?" He raised his arm high over his head. "Well, could I?"

Murdock donned a patronizing grin. He placed a warm hand on Sanders' arm. "Bill, did your arm move just then? I mean, did you perceive it to move?"

"Of course."

"But I tell you that it did not move. It cannot move, since it is taped to your chest. You just thought it moved. You imagined it. That is what the drug is doing to you. It has not only obliterated all pain, it has obliterated all knowledge of what may be causing pain. Your mind has been dissociated from your brain."

Sanders shook his head. "You're wrong, Doctor. There's nothing wrong with me."

"You're the one who is wrong, Bill. But let's not argue now. You get some rest, and I'll come back later and we'll talk. We have to study this some more. We have to learn more about this drug."

"If it's the drug that you're worrying about," Sanders said, "Why don't you just stop giving it to me?"

Murdock looked like a man with infinite wisdom. "We did stop giving it to you. In fact, you were given only one injection. You are not now, nor have you been since I operated on you, under any medication other than standard antibiotics. And you're still broken up like a rag doll."

"You, Doctor, are crazy."

"If I am, then so is the whole world."

          *   *   *   *   *

"I'm telling you that the drug is working," shouted Jenkins.

"And I'm telling you that it's working too well,"

retorted Murdock. "It has healed his body but taken away his mind. You should have seen him, feebly shaking his elbow because his arm was tied to his chest, and telling me that he was raising it straight up. And he wasn't just joking. He truly believed that he was doing it. It's gruesome. I just hope that the drug wears off. He seems to be living in a permanent hallucination. It's as though he were high on a mind expansion drug."

"The mice never came down. Of course, they never showed any signs of being high. They just went about their business while their bodies healed. They showed no pain at all, and no interest other than in food."

"And how were their mating habits?"

"Nonexistent. They ignored everything else around them, including other mice. The only thing they took notice of was food."

"Then so far, Bill is acting just like a mouse. At least he eats. But I wish we had some idea of knowing how long it was before the mice regained their memory."

"Mice don't really demonstrate memory, unless they're trained. And these were ordinary laboratory mice. They live instinctively, and they carried on that way after injection of the drug. But it's because mice don't think that we had to have a human experimenter. We needed someone who could provide feedback – who could tell us what was going on. Bill is giving us valuable information."

"Bill is a mental vegetable; a man without a mind; an experiment that has backfired."

"But we don't know for certain that the drug had anything to do with his present mental state."

"Since when did you become a doctor?" Murdock said ruthlessly. "You're a research biochemist, and although that gives you some medical knowledge, it does not entitle you to make diagnoses. There is something wrong with Sanders, and it must be related to the drug. He did not suffer any brain damage in the accident."

Jenkins was unruffled by the chastisement. "In any case, give it some time before you make any hasty deductions. That's a premise which I am qualified to make. Observation before deduction."

"We're not dealing with a lab rat, Don. We're dealing with a patient – and a friend."

Bill Sanders chose that moment to walk into the conference room. He stared out from clear painless eyes, and stood on both feet. He waved his arms in front of him. "So you both profess to be my friends. And the woman says that she's my wife. And I'm supposed to be injured. I must say that I find this hoax is becoming more preposterous by the minute."

"*Bill,*" Murdock screamed. He and Don both jumped up and rushed to Sanders' side. "What the hell are you doing out of bed? You can't walk on that leg yet."

Before Sanders had the opportunity to protest, they grabbed him and eased him onto the tabletop while Murdock bellowed for a nurse. It was Marion who answered the call.

"Oh, Bill," she cried.

"I'll go get a stretcher," Jenkins said, on his way out the door.

"Bill, you shouldn't have. You'll hurt yourself."

"I'm telling you people that I feel fine."

"Of course you do," Murdock agreed. "That's the drug cutting out all symptoms of pain. But it will not aid your broken bones if you persist in agitating them. You must exercise intellectual awareness of your actual condition."

"And I'm telling you that I have no broken limbs. Now let me go."

Sanders struggled to rise, but Jenkins arrived with a gurney, and both he and Murdock wrestled Sanders onto the padded mattress and strapped him down.

"Let go of me, will you? I tell you I'm all right."

"Bill, stop it!" Marion pleaded. "Stop it, I tell you."

Sanders protested loudly, but the men succeeded in transporting him to his room with the help of a couple of strong-armed orderlies who were used to violent patients. They transferred him to his bed and strapped him down with difficulty. Sanders screamed like the devil, but they paid him no mind. Murdock re-affixed the traction rig.

*   *   *   *   *

After the orderlies departed, the three of them talked in the corridor outside of Sanders private room.

"George, Don, will one of you please tell me what's going to happen to him? I'm scared."

"Now, my dear," Murdock said soothingly. "Take it easy. Everything will be all right. But we need some time to study his case. Bill is in an abnormal state of mind, and until we discover the limitations of this drug, we can't know any more about how it will continue to affect him. Time will be our best guide."

"But I want to know now," Marion cried. She leaned against Jenkins' shoulder.

Jenkins said to Murdock, "I suppose now you'll say that the drug gave him abnormal strength."

"No. I would only venture to stay that, since it is obviously doing its job so well by concealing all sensation of pain, he was able to walk on the broken leg without realizing that he could be doing himself damage. There is a reason for feeling some pain, if just to remind the patient that he is hurt. Why don't you take Marion to the cafeteria and get her some coffee. I think I'll have a little chat with Bill, after he has calmed down."

"How about administering a sedative?"

Murdock shook his head. "I'm afraid to prescribe any kind of tranquilizer. I don't know what kind of cumulative effect it might have with your ultimate analgesic. The brain receptors . . . " His voice trailed off. He was talking to himself, lost in thought.

After Jenkins and Marion left, George Murdock stepped quietly into Sanders' room.

Sanders looked at him sullenly. "There's no sense in hiding it from me any longer, Doctor. I know where I am. I'm in a private sanatorium – an insane asylum."

"That's not strictly true," Murdock said, pulling a chair next to the bed. "It's true that you are in an institution, as I prefer to think of it, but it is not private. It is government funded."

"A rose by any other name . . . " Sanders quoted.

"Quite true, but you belong here."

"I'm not crazy," Sanders screamed.

"That isn't quite what I meant. You belong here because you work here. You are a psychiatrist. You are the resident, and your wife is a psychiatric nurse. The head nurse, as it happens."

"Don't play up to me."

"I'm not. I'm telling you the truth. You are one of the foremost authorities on schizophrenia. You have been experimenting with drug-induced methods of relieving schizophrenia, and you and Don Jenkins have been working together to discover more powerful combatants for this dread disease."

Doubt clouded Sanders' mind.

"I work here too. I am your colleague, although I am more of a surgeon and medical practitioner. I've known you for many years. Since before you were married."

"Don't try to make me believe that that woman is my wife."

"She is, and she loves you very much. That's why she's so worried about you."

"It's not true. She's just a nurse – part of your game to make me believe that I'm crazy."

"Nobody thinks you're crazy. But you *are* under the influence of a new and hitherto untried drug."

Sanders humphed. "An unlikely story."

"But sadly, a true one."

"And where did this new drug come from?"

Murdock was pleased that Sanders was at last showing some interest – in anything. "As a matter of fact, you developed it." He let the meaning of that sink in before he continued. "You and Don Jenkins, that is. You've been creating new drugs for several years now, with varying amounts of success. Don is a research bio-chemist. The two of you have been working very close-ly to develop new compounds for the treatment of schiz-ophrenia. You tell him which effect the various drugs have had on your patients, and he alters the molecular structure in order to achieve stronger and more effective treatments.

"Serendipitously, you found that some of the drugs reduce or eliminate physical pain by operating synergistically with natural endorphins that block the pain receptors in the brain. The effect this has on schizophrenics has yet to be determined, because individual sufferers cannot be used as test subjects until the drugs have been tested in the laboratory on nonhuman subjects, such as mice.

"What you are attempting to prove is that schizophrenia can be treated by dissociating a patient from pain – both physical and emotional. Your success has been remarkable. This latest drug, however, suppresses so much of the pain centers that, it appears, absolutely no stimuli breach the receptors in the brain.

"At first this seemed like a perfect solution to schizophrenia, as well as a universal sedative, analgesic, and global anesthetic. In fact, I did not operate on you until after Don administered your latest test drug – without my knowledge, I might add. I would never have approved it. Once the administration was a fait accompli, I undertook the necessary surgical procedures that were necessary to set your broken bones. You performed extremely well under surgery, without any other anesthetic. I must admit that I have great hopes for this drug, if only we can work out the bugs . . . "

Sanders' interest was piqued. "Which are?"

"So far, it appears, total loss of all memories that comprise the personality. Complete dissociation from reality. In short, amnesia, but it goes much deeper than that. By way of example, you don't remember anything from your past."

"You're wrong, Doctor. I don't care."

"How can you not care who you are? How can you not be the least bit curious? How can you not show emotion over such a tremendous loss of individuality?"

"Because none of that is important. It matters little to me what I was yesterday, or what you say I was yesterday. What matters is now. I am now what I am. I start from here. That past life to which you allude is inconsequential to me. It is irrelevant.

"Don't say that to your wife."

"Forget her. I have. She is nothing to me."

"And I? Am I nothing to you?"

Nodding, Sanders said, "That's right, Doctor. All of you are nothing. The only thing that is meaningful to me is what I am."

"Or what you perceive yourself to be."

"It amounts to the same thing."

"No, it doesn't. Because what you perceive yourself to be is not what I perceive you to be. To me you are a sick patient. To Marion you are a helpless husband. To Don you are a research subject. You are all these things to all these people."

"Your perceptions don't matter to me," Sanders insisted. "Only my perceptions count. I perceive myself to be me, what I see before me, and what I see in the mirror of my mind. All else is fakery. You are fake. You don't even exist in my frame of reference."

Murdock sighed. "This discussion is getting a little to philosophical for me. Your perceptions are induced by a powerful chemical agent. They are not real. They are just figments of your imagination, or hallucinations, much like a misguided trip on lysergic acid diethylamide. The particular derivative you are working on now produces peculiar delusions, I admit, but these delusions seem real only to you, inside your mind. Delusions cannot be externalized."

"What is reality other than what one perceives it to be?"

"Again, you delve in philosophy: an exercise in solipsism. I am dealing with unalterable facts."

"Facts are relative to truth and to the perception of truth."

"Facts are immutable. Whether you choose to believe in them or not, they exist. A bullet through the head will kill you whether or not you believe in it. You must accept that."

"Why? Because you tell me so? I perceive only what *I* perceive, not what *you* perceive or want me to believe."

"You will only hurt yourself by persisting in such a notion. You think you have no injuries. Let me ask you again. What do you see when you look at yourself? Do you see a hopeless cripple, bound in a cast, wrapped in tape, slung in traction?"

"No. I see me as a healthy person in perfect physical condition."

"Then I must protect you from your own delusions, Bill. For your own good. I hate to do this, but I must keep you in restraints until you forget these fanciful if comfortable delusions."

Sanders stared, but without any show of hostility.

Murdock rose from his chair. On his way out the door, he turned sadly and said, "Bill, despite what you say about perception, no matter how you look at reality, it won't change simply because you don't like it the way it is. You can delude yourself into believing anything you want, but that doesn't make it so. Now, please get a good night's sleep. Your body needs the rest. Good night."

Murdock closed the door behind him.

Bill Sanders had no intention of resting. He held his arm – the one that Murdock said was broken – in front of his face. As far as he could see, there was nothing wrong with it. He did not believe there was, so there was not. Neither did he believe that his body was bound by straps – and it was not. He rose from the bed, walked across the room, and slipped through the door.

He did not know whether or not to believe all of Murdock's fancy stories. He might really have been a psychiatrist at one time. But the past made no difference to him any more. He was today not the person he had been yesterday. He held to no known precepts. He just was.

He walked along the spotless corridor, down the metal staircase, and through a side door into the night-time stillness. Outside it was cold – bitterly cold. In fact, it was snowing. But he could feel no pain from the cold, because his new mind did not believe in pain. He understood, however, that he was trapped.

That he stood inside a fenced asylum was irrelevant. But he was trapped in a physical corporeality that had no essence in his new life.

He had to escape. He ran.

He ran across the hospital grounds, through the trees and over the neatly trimmed lawn. He was unencumbered by broken limbs or plaster casts. He reached a fence. It rose ten feet high, and was spiked on top. No one was there to tell him that he could not climb it. He hit the diamond crosshatches with fingers and toes. Then he was standing in the snow on the other side of the fence. He had escaped from the asylum.

The sound of a crash came from behind him. A door had burst open in the building. There was a rectangular spot of light, and framed in it momentarily, one at a time, were three figures: two men and one woman. The white snow created an abnormal amount of brightness due to reflection from the moon. The people must have spotted him outside the fence, for there arose a simultaneous triad of shouts.

Sanders turned away and ran. That he could be caught never entered his consciousness; ergo, he could not be caught.

Don Jenkins, the youngest of the trio that chased after Sanders, reached the fence first. He could not believe what he saw: footprints ending on one side of the fence, and continuing on the other side. It was impossible for anyone to have scaled a fence like that – for the top was electrified.

Breathless, George Murdock and Marion Sanders stopped beside Jenkins.

"I don't know how the hell he got over," Jenkins declared. "It's impossible."

"This is even more impossible," Murdock said, pointing at the naked footprints in the snow. "Somehow he's managed to shed his cast and run – *run* – on a compound fracture. He's got the strength of a madman. We've got to stop him before he does irreparable damage to himself."

"George, Don, you've got to do something," Marion

cried. She was only lightly dressed – too lightly for the winter conditions then prevailing.

None of them wore coats.

"You run along this fence till you reach the gate," Jenkins explained hurriedly. "I'll go back and get the side gate key." He was off, without waiting for a reply.

It was the only logical thing to do, so Murdock and Marion did what he suggested. Minutes later, Jenkins arrived with the key, breathing hard now, for he had raced all the way to the main office and back. He opened the gate and they filed through in a rush, leaving the gate open behind them. They ran along the fence until they reached the naked footprints, then they tracked him through the woods that surrounded the asylum.

Up ahead, Bill Sanders was not even thinking of pursuit. He was too occupied in experiencing his new actualization. As a result, he was caught unawares when the three figures dashed out of the protection of the trees, and shone a flashlight on him. He zoomed away, and the three figures ran after him.

Sanders was fast – as fast as he wanted to be. In his new perception of reality, there were no limits to what he could do. There were no known natural laws. He simply made them up as he went along. Every second was unprecedented, unbound by anything from his past. He did not live on accepted theory – he created theory as he passed through time.

The forest ended, and there was open rock ahead of him. He moved along the loose scree, not knowing what was in front of him. He did not see the cliff until he had reached it. He had time to stop, but the three pursuers nearly caught up with him before he could decide how best to proceed. They were only fifty feet behind him, emerging from the tree line.

Since no one in his newborn essence had ever told him that he could not fly, he jumped off the edge.

At first he soared with the wind, free as the breeze. But then his fledgling body commenced to be dragged down inexorably to some far-off center of gravity of which he was only peripherally aware – until he realized that gravity had a material affect on his physical body.

That did not mean that he could not fly – it simply meant that he had to get rid of everything that was attracted to the meager force of gravity: mass. For mass possessed weight. He had to shed that mass in order to fly. His body was dragging him down to the ground far below.

As he fell, he struggled to rid himself of his massive encumbrance. He shed his hospital pajamas in free fall, but it was not enough. Just before he struck the ground, he felt his mind lurch free. Then he soared up into the air – up into the world that only he could perceive, into his perception of reality, while those earthbound creatures who were mired in their ideas and preconceived notions, plodded slowly along the ground.

"It's an abandoned quarry," Don said hopelessly.

"Oh, my god," Marion cried. She fell against Murdock, who tried to comfort her.

"I'm sorry, Marion. I'm so sorry. I don't know how it happened. When I left him, he was strapped securely to the bed. I don't know how he got loose. He must have squirmed out somehow, because the straps were still in place and the buckles were still buckled."

"Stop offering condolences," Don snapped. "Let's get down to the bottom of this cliff. There's a chance that he survived the fall."

They ran along the top edge of the drop off. In due course, they found an old trucking road that led down to the bottom. They ran down the road and back to the point at which Sanders' body had struck the bedrock.

His broken body lay in a heap. His bandages were torn, his cast was shattered. His neck was broken. He was dead.

Marion knelt beside him and cradled his bloody head. She whimpered. Off to one side, Murdock and Jenkins conversed in low tones, gripping their teeth against the cold.

"We'll never know what was going through his mind in those final minutes," Murdock noted sadly.

Jenkins breathed a sigh that was almost a gasp. He was overcome by remorse. "I realize now that we should have been more cautious with that drug."

Murdock found the strength to be forgiving. "Don't blame yourself, Don. The drug did was it was supposed to do. Bill died painlessly."

"Sure. The operation was a success but the patient died."

While all three people fumbled with their personal pangs of regret, they were totally unaware of the greater event that was occurring far above them.

High overhead, swooping delicately through the air, an unbound entity passed into a new existence that was yet unexplored by man, heading upward, ever outward, past the moon, past the planets, and, assuming faster-than-light speeds, past the stars and out of the galaxy into the infinite heavens beyond.